# Annotated Japanese Literary Gems

日本文学ルビ付き名作叢書

多和田葉子　林京子　中上健次

# Annotated Japanese Literary Gems

*Stories by*

Tawada Yōko

Hayashi Kyōko

Nakagami Kenji

Volume One

*Selected and edited by*

Kyoko Selden

Jolisa Gracewood

East Asia Program
Cornell University
Ithaca, New York 14853

*The Cornell East Asia Series is published by the Cornell University East Asia Program (distinct from Cornell University Press). We publish affordably priced books on a variety of scholarly topics relating to East Asia as a service to the academic community and the general public. Standing orders, which provide for automatic notification and invoicing of each title in the series upon publication, are accepted.*

*If after review by internal and external readers a manuscript is accepted for publication, it is published on the basis of camera-ready copy provided by the volume author. Each author is thus responsible for any necessary copy-editing and for manuscript formatting. Address submission inquiries to CEAS Editorial Board, East Asia Program, Cornell University, Ithaca, New York 14853-7601.*

Number 130 in the Cornell East Asia Series
Copyright © 2006 by Kyoko Selden and Jolisa Gracewood. All rights reserved
ISSN 1050-2955
ISBN-13: 978-1-885445-33-9 hc / ISBN-10: 1-885445-33-4 hc (Volume 1)
ISBN-13: 978-1-885445-30-8 pb / ISBN-10: 1-885445-30-X pb (Volume 1)
ISBN-13: 978-1-933947-00-6 set / ISBN-10: 1-933947-00-4 set (Multi-volume set)
Library of Congress Control Number: 2006923154
Printed in the United States of America
24 23 22 21 20 19 18 17 16 15 14 13 12 11 10 09 06 9 8 7 6 5 4 3 2 1

Cover illustration from a Japanese stencil, late 19th or early 20th century, Herbert F. Johnson Museum of Art, Cornell University, gift of Drs. Lee and Constance Koppelman. Cover design by Karen K. Smith.

♾ The paper in this book meets the requirements for permanence of ISO 9706:1994.

CAUTION: Except for brief quotations in a review, no part of this book may be reproduced or utilized in any form without permission in writing from the author. Please address inquiries to Kyoko Selden in care of the East Asia Program, Cornell University, 140 Uris Hall, Ithaca, NY 14853-7601.

# Contents

Preface ... vii

TAWADA YŌKO ... 1
- About Tawada Yōko ... 2
- Readers on the Train ... 4
- A Dictionary Village ... 12
- A Town Called Z ... 19

HAYASHI KYŌKO ... 27
- About Hayashi Kyōko ... 28
- My Friend ... 30

NAKAGAMI KENJI ... 49
- About Nakagami Kenji ... 50
- Trees and Grass ... 52

Plain Texts
- Readers on the Train ... 67
- A Dictionary Village ... 73
- A Town Called Z ... 79
- My Friend ... 85
- Trees and Grass ... 99

# Annotated Japanese Literary Gems

Annotated Japanese Literary Gems makes available representative examples of short stories and novellas from Meiji to contemporary days. The collection provides *rubi* transliterations for almost all kanji except when the same kanji recurs. Together with extensive annotations explaining advanced vocabulary, syntax and grammar, and social or historical context, the transliterated texts serve as a resource for students of modern Japanese literature.

*Rubi* is a printing term from "ruby," the English 5.5 point font, which is approximately the size of the small kana used to assist readers of newspapers, fiction, and scripture. The centuries-old convention of adding small kana to provide the pronunciation of kanji was widely practiced in modern printed texts beginning in Meiji, until Japan's postwar Ministry of Education drastically reduced the number of kanji for official and general use and called for the elimination of *rubi* from most publications.

The virtues of *rubi* are demonstrated by two recent examples. Yanase Naoki's translation of James Joyce's *Finnegans Wake* (I and II in 1997; expanded to I-IV in 2004) makes imaginative use of *rubi*, evoking late-Edo and early Meiji playful use of *rubi* as part of the exuberant word play that is present throughout the novel. In Senoo Kappa's autobiographical novel, *Shōnen H* (The Boy Called H, two volumes, 1997), *rubi* makes the wartime episodes with obsolescent kanji compounds accessible to children and others of the postwar generations. In a brief prefatory note, Senoo explains why he used *rubi* in his text: "In the old books every kanji came with *rubi*, so [as a child] I was able to read books meant for adults and learn kanji in the process." Children nowadays still pick up kanji from juvenile books with *rubi*, but in the past, they had effortlessly learned to recognize a vastly larger number of kanji from fiction and newspapers.

*Rubi* is invaluable in Japanese language learning for non-native speakers. Looking up kanji and words is important for developing kanji-Japanese and Japanese-Japanese dictionary skills; it can also be fun. Constant dictionary work focused on single expressions, however, not only slows readers but impedes their observation of other elements crucial to full comprehension of a text: how words are connected, how sentences are constructed, how a passage follows a train of thought, whose voice the line represents, and in what tone a work is written. This series of annotated texts is intended to save heavy dictionary work and assist the reader to appreciate expressions in context rather than concentrating on kanji and vocabulary that are accessed elsewhere.

A small number of bilingual and annotated Japanese language textbooks already exist. Kodansha's Bilingual Books, which notably includes *Key Words in the News* (1998), is one example. Annotated *rubi* editions of literary sources are rare, however. This collection, with full *rubi* and informative annotations, may contribute to a broadening of the range of materials accessible to intermediate and advanced Japanese students interested in language, literature, culture and society. It drew inspiration from annotated language and literature editions used at the college level in Japan, as well as from similar European mini-volumes. Although these usually contain a single piece per volume, as a general rule, we combine two or three authors so that each volume introduces more than one theme, style, and level of linguistic challenge.

For each story, the text with *rubi* appears on the right page and annotations on the left. Paragraphs (or groups of paragraphs where individual paragraphs are extremely brief) are numbered to facilitate locating annotations. A brief note on the author precedes each text. At the end of the volume, plain text versions in a smaller font without *rubi* are attached. Abbreviations within the annotations are as follows: *no.* (note), *lit.* (literally), *hist.* (historical, history), *onomat.* (onomatopeia), *mod. J.* (modern Japanese), and *Ch.* (Chinese).

## VOLUME ONE

This first volume of the Annotated Japanese Literary Gems introduces stories by three important postwar authors: Tawada Yōko, who lives in Hamburg and publishes both in German and Japanese with insight into how individual languages and the spaces between them work; Hayashi Kyōko, a Nagasaki author who spent her childhood years in wartime Shanghai and has written about both a-bomb and colonial experiences; and Nakagami Kenji, a native of Shingū in Wakayama, and the first Japanese author to identify himself as burakumin, who concentrated on the themes of burakumin and their heritage. Forthcoming volumes highlight the writings of Natsume Sōseki, Inoue Yasushi, Tomioka Taeko, Akutagawa Ryūnosuke, Tanizaki Junichirō, and Tsushima Yūko.

Jolisa and I would like to thank Karen Brazell, Brett de Bary, Joan Piggott, and John Whitman for their encouragement and counsel over the years; Yuki Furuya and Ryu Iwase for their diligent word processing assistance in the pre-scanner days when this project began; Lili Selden for valued comments on the annotations; students in Cornell University's Japanese reading courses for sharing our enthusiasm with stories such as these; and Karen Smith for professional editing and formatting guidance. The project was partially supported by the Consortium of Language Teaching and Learning directed by Peter Patrikis, to whom thanks are also due. More personally, Tsukamoto Tetsuzō's editing and annotating of pre-Meiji Japanese literature, such as the prewar Yūhōdō Library and the postwar *tsūkai* (annotated) series, has long been a source of inspiration.

K. S.

# 電車の中で本を読む人々
# 辞書の村
# Zという町

多和田葉子

# Readers on the Train
# A Dictionary Village
# A Town Called Z

*Tawada Yōko*

TAWADA YŌKO (1960- ) is among the first Japanese fiction writers to publish successfully both in Japanese and a European language. At age nineteen, while studying Russian literature at Waseda University, she toured Moscow, Warsaw, Berlin, Hamburg, and Frankfurt, where she experienced the alienating effect of foreign languages. She subsequently worked in Hamburg for several years at an export book company, and earned a Ph.D. from Zürich University in German literature in 2000. She has been a resident of Hamburg since 1982.

A writer from early youth, she began publishing professionally in 1987. *Nur da wo du bist da ist nichts* (Only where you are there is nothing, 1987) consists of one short story and nineteen poems with the original Japanese alternating with Peter Pörtner's German translations. Her Japanese works include *Kitsunetsuki* (Fox-possessed Moon, 1997, a collection of eighteen poetic prose pieces); "Kakato wo nakushite" (recipient of the 1991 Gunzō Literary Prize; tr. "Missing Heels," 1998); "Inumukoiri" (winner of the 1993 Akutagawa Prize; tr. "The Bridegroom Was a Dog," 1998); *Arufabetto no kizuguchi* (An Open Wound in the Alphabet, 1994); *Gottoharuto tetsudō* (The Gotthard Railway, 1997); *Seijo densetsu* (Legend of a Saintly Woman, a novel, 1996); *Hikon* (The Flying Spirit, a novel, 1998); *Hikari to zerachin no raipuchihhi* (Leipzig of Light and Gelatin, short stories, 2000). Tawada received the 28th Izumi Kyōka Literature Prize for *Hinagiku no ocha no baai* (When It's Chamomile, short stories, 2000) and the Tanizaki Jun'ichirō Prize for *Yōgisha no yakō-ressha* (The Suspect's Night Train, 2002). Reflecting Tawada's characteristic play with language, the original Japanese of *Das Bad* (1989, tr. Peter Pörtner) remains deliberately unpublished, while an English translation has been included in a recent publication.

Among Tawada's original German works are *Das Fremde aus der Dose* (1992, two stories, translated by Susan Bernofsky as "Canned Foreign" and "The Talisman"); *Die Kranichmaske, die bei Nacht strahlt* (The Cranemask, Which Radiates at Night, 1993, a stage play); *Ein Gast* (A Guest, 1993); *Aber die Mandarinen müssen heute abend noch geraubt werden* (But the Mandarins Must Still Be Stolen this Evening, 1996, a collection of prose poems); *Wie der Wind im Ei* (As the Wind in the Egg, 1996, a play); and *Überseezungen* (Foreign Tongues, 2002).

In 1996 she became the first Japanese recipient of the Adelbert von Chamisso Preis awarded for German-language writings by non-native German speakers. Tawada was a 1997 recipient of the Förderpreis für Literatur der Hansestadt Hamburg (Hamburg City Prize for Encouraging Literature) for her *Wo Europa anfängt* (Where Europe Begins, 1998) and other pieces. Since 1987, she has given numerous readings in literary salons, theatres, and universities in and out of Germany, notably in Japan and the US.

Tawada's major theme is language, and particularly alienation from language. Through her works of poetry, drama, and fiction, she examines language with the ear of a foreigner, plays with words and their ambiguities, discovers fresh meanings and examines the indeterminate space between languages.

Three pieces have been selected for this reader from *Kitsunetsuki*, a collection of eighteen poetic prose pieces. They introduce, respectively, commonplace urban subway scenes viewed with the bemused eye of a foreigner, a village made of words from a dictionary, and a dream visit to a longed-for place. Here, too, we find examples of Tawada's linguistic transgressions, which fracture commonly accepted, seemingly logical connections between words, objects, and ideas, and which create new logics in the illogical.

## WORKS IN ENGLISH TRANSLATION

From German, all by Susan Bernofsky:

"Zurich" (fiction, Zurich: Offzin/Kunsthaus, 1997).

"A 21st-Century Hurdy-Gurdy" (poem, *Yellow Silk* 48, 1995)

*Where Europe Begins*. Susan Bernofsky, tr. (New Directions, 2002).

From Japanese:

*The Bridegroom Was a Dog*. Margaret Mitsutani, tr. (short story collection, Tokyo: Kodansha International, 1998.)

"Stars Scintillating in the Eyes." Kyoko Selden tr., *Review of Japanese Culture and Society* (Center for Inter-Cultural Studies and Education, Josai University, December 2001).

"The Bath" and "Spores." Yumi Selden tr., in *Where Europe Begins*.

### 場所

**この町** *A recurring expression in Tawada's work. Here the narrator, a returnee from abroad, observes with fresh interest the reading habits of train riders in a Japanese city.* **唯一の** the only. **電車の中では、人は名前がないので、時間がたっぷりある** on the train, people have no names so they have plenty of time—*Logical leaps like this are characteristic of Tawada's writing.*

### 仮面

**仮面** mask. **癖** habit, quirk, foible. **隠す** to hide; to conceal. **本は顔を隠すためにあるのかと思ってしまうほどだ** I almost think that books exist for the purpose of hiding faces. **本は……仮面のようなものかもしれない** a book [read on the train in this manner] may be something like a mask that gives a second name and a title to one who reads it. *When the reader's face is covered by the book, other passengers can only see the author's name and the book title.*

# 電車の中で読書する人々

## 場所

この町の人たちは、家では本を読まない。図書館でも本を読まない。電車だけが読書の唯一の場所なのである。電車の中では、人は名前がないので、時間がたっぷりある。

## 仮面

電車の中で本を読む人たちには変な癖がたくさんある。たとえば、本を鼻に近づけすぎる。本は顔を隠すためにあるのかと思ってしまうほどだ。本は、それを読む人の顔に、第二の名前とひとつのタイトルを与える仮面のようなものかもしれない。

**嗅覚**

**たちのぼる** to rise up (mist, fragrance, etc). **においをかぐ** to sniff; smell. *A sleeper with a book still open and perhaps held close to his nose looks, because of his deep respiration, as if inhaling the smell rising from the lettering on the pages.*

**手話**

**手話** sign language. **支える** to support. **内容** the contents, text. **人間には理解できない会話** (fingers carry forward) dialogues incomprehensible to humans [to whom the fingers belong]. **勝手に** as one pleases, wilfully. **進める** to advance; proceed with. **電車の中で交わされる**（交される）**隠語のようなもの** something like a secret language exchanged on the train.

**釣り人**

**釣り人** angler, fisherman. **右手の人さし指を耳の穴に突っ込んで** with the right index finger thrust into the ear. **声を聞かないですむように** so as not to have to hear voices (other than the one heard from within the book). **時たま** once in a (long) while; at long intervals; たまに. **記憶** memory. **釣り上げる** to fish up. **釣竿** fishing pole. **その人さし指は……** On occasion, that index finger turns into a fishing pole that reels in a memory from the depths of the ear.

**重層構造**

**重層構造** multi-layered construction. **日の光が本の表面にさす** the sunlight hits the pages. **樹木** trees (and shrubs). *The kanji 樹 refers to big trees.* **右から左へ滑っていく** [as the train moves] (the shadow of the trees on the pages) glides from right to left. **文字は上から下へと流れる** the lettering [on the pages] streams from top to bottom.

### 嗅覚

本を読みながら眠ってしまった人は、文字から立ちのぼってくるにおいをかいでいるようにもみえる。

### 手話

本を支えている指の形は、ひとりひとり違っている。指は何かを言おうとしている。それは本の内容とも関係がないし、読んでいる人の性格とも関係がない。指たちは、人間には理解できない会話を勝手に進めている。その手話は、電車の中で交わされる隠語のようなものだ。

### 釣り人

右手の人さし指を耳の穴に突っ込んで、本を読んでいる人もいる。本の中から聞こえてくる声以外の声を聞かないですむように。その人さし指は時たま、耳の奥から記憶を釣り上げる釣竿となる。

### 重層構造

日の光が本の表面にさし、樹木のかげが右から左へ滑っていく。文字は上から下へと流れる。樹木と文字がページの上で正面衝突を起こすことはない。だから、本の表面にはいくつもの層があるのだ

**正面衝突** head-on collision, frontal clash. **だから、本の表面にはいくつもの層があるのだということが分かる** So, this makes you realize that there are many layers on the book surface. *A reasoning typical of Tawada. The shadow of the trees runs from right to left because the trees pass by as the train moves, while the lettering runs up and down as the eyes follow the vertical lines of the text. The shadow and the lettering are not expected to collide. The narrator surprises the commonsensical logic by likening them to two substantial objects, one moving horizontally and the other vertically, and anticipating a collision. Then she mentions her discovery that there is no collision, and concludes that, therefore, the surface of an open book is multi-structured.*

**謎**

**謎** mystery, riddle, enigma. **角度** angle. **頭をちょっと傾げるたびに** each time [the child] tilts its head slightly. **微笑みが浮かぶ** a smile surfaces [on its lips]. **とどまる** to stop, rest, grind to a halt. **頭を少し動かすだけで、違う物語が現れるらしい** just a little tilt of the head and a new story seems to emerge.

**覗き**

**覗き** peeping, from 覗く, to peep. **好奇心** curiosity. **抑える** to suppress, rein in, keep in check. **まるで……とでも言うように** as much as to say that [she is unable to suppress her curiosity unless she does that, i.e., tries not to turn her eyes toward the book]. **盗み読み** from 盗み読む, to read surreptitiously, to read over someone's shoulder. **電車に乗っている人間のすることの中で最も恥ずかしいことだとされている** is considered the most shameful act of all the things people do on trains. **覗き魔** Peeping Tom; voyeur; snoop. **(〜の)興味を引く** to attract the interest (of 〜). **普通なら絶対読まないような本** books that one would never read under ordinary circumstances.

ということが分かる。

## 謎

子供が、本のページをいろいろな角度から眺めている。頭をちょっと傾げるたびに、くちびるに微笑みが浮かぶ。子供は先へ進もうとはせず、同じページにとどまったままだ。頭を少し動かすだけで、違う物語が現れるらしい。

## 覗き

本を読む人の右隣りにすわっている女は、本の方を見ないようにしている。まるでそうしなければ好奇心を抑えることができないとでも言うように、女は右の方ばかり見ている。隣にすわっている人の本を盗み読みするのは、電車に乗っている人間のすることの中でもっとも恥ずかしいことだとされている。誰でも、覗き魔だとは思われたくない。同じ本を図書館で見たとしたら、興味を引かれなかったかもしれない。電車に乗っていると、誰でも、普通なら絶対読まないような本にまで興味を感じる。

## 広がり

電車がどんなに混んでいても、本さえ読んでいれば狭くてやりきれないということはない。本のペー

### 広がり

**広がり** an expanse; a broad sweep. **どんなに混んでいても** no matter how crowded it is. **本さえ読んでいれば** so long as / if only one is reading. **狭くてやりきれないということはない** one never feels unbearably squeezed in. **無限の空間** infinite / limitless space.

### 連帯感

**連帯感** a feeling of solidarity. **羊** sheep. **押しつけあう** to press up against each other; huddle together. **口をきかず** (from 口をきく) without talking; in silence. **ますます** increasingly; all the more.

### 未練

**未練** lingering affection. **ページをめくったばかりの子どもの人さし指** the index finger of a child who has just turned the page. **ページに張り付いたまま、離れようとしない** [the index finger] remains stuck to the page [that the child has already read], refusing to detach itself. **視線は先へと進むのに** although the eyes move ahead [on the page]. **指はいつまでもそこにとどまっている** the finger stays there forever. **展開する** to develop, unfold. **話がよいほうに……** Though aware that the story will develop in a happier direction, the child cannot bring herself to move on from a sad passage.

### 統合

**制服** school uniform. **統合** integration; unification; consolidation. **誰も本の高さなど気にしていない** (気にしていない from 気にする) nobody is concerned about the height of the books; i.e., the children hold their books at the same height not because they are trying to do so.

ジが、読書する人のまわりに無限の空間を拡げる。

## 連帯感

子供たちが、羊のように身体を押しつけあいながら立っている。どの子供も自分の本を読んでいる。子供たちは口をきかず、ますます強く身体を押し付けあいながら読んでいる。

## 未練

ページをめくったばかりの子供の人さし指が、もう読んでしまったページに張り付いたまま、離れようとしない。視線は先へと進むのに、指はいつまでもそこにとどまっている。その文章を忘れるのが嫌なのだ。話が好いほうに展開していくのだと分かっていても、悲しい文章から離れる気になれないのだ。

## 統合

制服を着た五人の子供たちは、みんな同じ高さに本を支えている。誰も本の高さなど気にしていない。子供たちではなく、本たちがお互いを見つめあい、連帯しているのだ。その統一は、人間が無理やり足並みを揃えようとする時のように、ぎこちなかったり、冷酷であったりはしない。

**連帯する** to share solidarity; link up; join hands. **統一** unity. **無理やり** forcibly, against one's will. **足並みを揃える** to fall into step with, act in concert with. **ぎこちない**（*alt.* ぎごちない）stiff-legged, ungainly, awkward. **冷酷な** cruel, heartless.

**夢**

**主人公** main character, protagonist. **偶然** by chance. **以前どこかで会ったことがあるような気がして、おやっと思う** [the person who took a nap on the train] feels with a sense of surprise as if he has previously met [that character] somewhere. *The interjection「おやっ」varies in emphasis from "Goodness me!" to "Hmm," to "Huh?"*

**硬質**

**硬質** firmness, hardness, rigidity. **肌** skin; flesh. **真珠** pearl. **首飾り** necklace. **指輪** ring. **増す** to increase.

**飛翔**

**飛翔** flight; soaring [to / through the sky]. **（〜に）つかまる** to hold on (to 〜). Books have no place to hold on to, i.e., books can only be unsteadily held in people's hands, while people can hold on to straps or poles on the train. **空中** space, midair. **浮く** to float, bob about. **自分のあるべき高さを見つけることができずに** unable to find the right height for themselves. あるべき means "should be / ought to be / to be expected to be," or "right / ideal"; できずに is negative adverbial from できる.

## 夢

本を読む人の隣で居眠りすると、その本の主人公に夢の中で出会うことがある。居眠りしていたその人が、ある日どこかで偶然同じ本を読むと、初めて読む本なのに、主人公に以前どこかで会ったことがあるような気がして、おやっと思う。

## 硬質

本を読みながら肌が石のようになっていく女がいる。すると、目も鼻も口も閉じて、顔の中へゆっくりと消えていく。真珠の首飾りと指輪だけが輝きを増していく。

## 飛翔

電車の中で読まれる本は、つかまるところがない。机の上に置かれているのではなく、空中に浮いている。自分のあるべき高さを見つけることができずに、上がったり下がったりしていることもある。

## 祈り

電車の中で読まれる本が小さい時は両手が背表紙のところで組み合わされ、読んでいる人は、そん

### 祈り

**祈り** prayer.　**背表紙** dustjacket.　**両手を組み合わせる** to bring together one's hands; join palms.　**神々** the gods.　**捧げる** to offer (e.g. 祈りを神に).

### どこか

**視線** gaze.　**活字** typeface, letters.　**さまよう** to ramble, roam, wander.　**透明人間** invisible beings (透明 transparent;「透明人間」The Invisible Man). In the eyes of one reading a book, other passengers look like no more than invisible beings. **視線がさまよってきた空間** the space through which the gaze has wandered [is not inside the train but in a totally different place].

### 眼球

**眼球** eyeball.　**保護する** to protect.　**まつ毛がいつもより長くなる** [while one is reading, in order to protect / conceal eyeball movements from other people] one's eyelashes become longer than usual.　**目の脇の小皺** fine lines at the corners of the eyes; crowfeet wrinkles.　**目の脇の小じわが現れたり消えたりするので、視覚器官が働いていることが分かる** Because the crowfeet wrinkles come and go, one can tell that the [reader's] visual organ is working.

なつもりはないのに、お祈りしているような格好をすることになる。本が鼻の高さにある時は祈りは天の神々に捧げられ、お腹の高さにある時は地の神々に捧げられる。

## どこか

視線がちょっと活字を離れることもある。視線は空中をさまよい、何も見ることができないまま、本のところへどもってくる。他の乗客たちなどというものは、本を読んでいる人の目には、透明人間のようにしか見えない。視線がさまよってきた空間は、電車の中にあるのではなく、どこか全く別のところにある。

## 眼球

目の動きをまわりの人たちから保護するために、本を読んでいる間は、まつ毛がいつもより長くなる。目の玉は見えない。ただ、目の脇の小皺が現れたり消えたりするので、視覚器官が働いていることが分かる。

## 女と男

若い女達は、兵隊のように直立不動の姿勢で読書している。背広を着た会社員たちは大抵、上機嫌

### 女と男

**兵隊** soldier(s); troops. **直立不動の姿勢で** standing at attention. **背広** a business suit. **大抵** generally; in most cases; だいたいみな. **上機嫌の** good-humoured, cheerful. **背中をまるめる** to round one's shoulders, to be stoop-shouldered. **隣り合わせて** side by side. **背筋を伸ばして** with a straight back. **猫背** stoop shouldered. **くちびるひとつ動かさない** do not even once move their lips. **あたしたち、降りないと**（降りないといけない）We have to get off. 降りないと is short for 降りないといけない, (*lit.*) we must get off or it's no good.

**隣で本を読んでいるのが自分の妻であることを思い出す** (hearing her say this, the man) recalls that the person reading next to him is his wife. *An interesting way of looking at his oblivion. Note that the line says the man, absorbed in reading, has forgotten not that his wife was reading by his side but that the reader seated next to him was his wife.*

### 高校生

**視線で尋ねる** to ask with one's gaze. **首を縦に振る** to nod. **首を横に振る** to shake one's head.

### 綱渡り

**綱渡り** tightrope walking. **痩せた** thin, skinny. **扉の取っ手** door knob / handle. **揺れる** to sway. **額** forehead. **汗の玉** beads of sweat. **浮かぶ** to float; bob up; surface; cf. 浮く.

の猫のように背中を丸めている。男女が隣り合わせてすわって本を読んでいる。女は背筋を伸ばしてすわり、男は猫背である。ふたりは、くちびるひとつ動かさない。電車が止まると、女は急に口を大きく開けて、あきれたように言う。あたしたち、降りないと。そういわれて、男は隣で本を読んでいるのが自分の妻であることを思い出す。

## 高校生

二人の高校生が一緒に一冊の本を読んでいる。片方が、ページをめくってもいいかと視線で尋ねる度に、もう片方は首を縦に振ったり横に振ったりする。彼らは、ベッドに並んで横たわっているようにも見える。本がベッドを思い出させるのは、本もベッドも夢をみる場所だからかもしれない。

## 綱渡り

痩せた男が片手で電車の扉の取っ手につかまって読書している。綱渡りの男の話でも読んでいるのだろう。ページをめくっている間も、身体が右へ左へと揺れる。額には、汗の玉が浮かんでいる。

## 眼鏡

年配の婦人が読書用眼鏡をかけて本を読んでいる。眼鏡のグラスはふたつの層に分かれている。下

**眼鏡**

**年配の** elderly, of advanced years. **読書用眼鏡** reading glasses. **ふたつの層に分かれている** divided into two layers, i.e., the glasses are bifocal. **下の層を通して見えるのは** what is seen through the lower portions of the glasses. **生き物のような活字** printed letters that are like living creatures. *活字 (printing type, movable type) is not only alive for the reader but the word also literally means "living letters."* **銅像のような乗客たち** passengers like bronze statues.

**変換**

**変換** change; conversion; a computer program term meaning kana/kanji transformation. **暴力** violence. **受け止める** to stop (a blow); to catch (a ball); to parry or fend off. **本はその視線を受け止めて、文字に変換する** in response to that gaze, the book transforms itself into written words.

**子ども**

**ごく** extremely; quite. **幼い** of tender age. **巨大な** enormous; colossal. **絵本** illustrated book; picture book for children. **テング**（天狗） flying goblin, i.e, a half-man, half-bird creature in Japanese folklore with a long beak or a long nose, wings, and shining eyes. **テンシ**（天使） angel. **それは、テングかテンシが翼を広げているところのように見える** It (the way a very young child holds an open, large picture book) looks like a tengu or an angel spreading his wings. **場所を空ける** to make space. **行為** activity; conduct.

の層を通して見えるのは生き物のような活字であり、上の層を通して見えるのは銅像のような乗客たちである。

## 変換

視線は暴力かもしれない。本はその視線を受け止めて、文字に変換する。

## 子ども

乗客の身体が小さければ小さいほど、その手の中にある本は大きい。大人の読んでいる本は、子どもの絵本に比べると、とても小さい。ごく幼い子どもが、巨大な絵本を開く。それは、テングかテンシが翼を広げているところのように見える。電車は込んでいたが、それでもまわりの大人たちはできる限り、開かれる絵本のために場所を空けてやった。本を読むという行為には、こんなにも広い場所が必要なのだ。

1. **暦を驚き騒がす教会の鐘** the church bell that shakes up the calendar. 驚き騒がす, causative of 驚き騒ぐ, to be startled into a sensation. 驚かし騒がす with two causatives would be a more common way to say the same. *The first sentence can be read as a full sentence ("The church bell rings at five in the morning") or as a sentence fragment ("At five in the morning when the church bell rings") leading to the next ("the wind clangs").* **がらんがらんと鳴る** to clang, clamour. *がらんがらんと functions pivotally, suggesting both 鐘が鳴る, がらんがらんと and がらんがらんと風が吹く.* **アラスカ鮭** Alaskan salmon; a play on sound in アラスカ and カラス. **頭でっかち** top-heavy. **樹木** trees. **ばらんばらんと(落ちる)** to scatter noisily. **振り落とされる** to be shaken / thrown off or down. **丼型の** bowl-shaped.

2. **出来事** an event; a happening. **突飛な物も驚くには値しない** even wild things are no occasion for surprise. **突飛な** wild, fantastic, extraordinary. **〜に値する** to merit, deserve, be worthy of 〜. **場違いな** out of place. **恥じる** to be ashamed, to blush. **単語** single words; here, entry words. **でてくる順番に** in order of appearance. *For example, "Alaska," "ambassador" (paragraph 3), "apple," followed by "beer" (paragraph 4) and "crow."* **抜ける** to come out or off; slip out. **蝉** cicada. **抜け殻** a snake's or insect's discarded skin. **秋雨** autumn rain. **濡れる** to be soaked or drenched. **飴** candy. **溶ける** to melt; dissolve. When all of the words slipped out of its belly, the dictionary became like the discarded skin of a cicada, and, wet in the ceaseless autumn rain that began falling the following day, it melted away like candy.

# 辞書の村

一

暦を驚き騒がす教会の鐘が鳴る朝の五時に。がらんがらんと風が吹く。アラスカ鮭やカラスや林檎が、頭でっかちの樹木の枝から、ばらんばらんと振り落とされる。やわらかい土に、丼型の穴が開く。

二

その村には出来事というほどの出来事もない。その村は辞書の中から生まれた。だから、その村では突飛な物も驚くには値しない。場違いであっても恥じる必要がない。辞書の中に出てくる単語たちが、でてくる順番に、現実のものになって、そうして村ができ上がった。村ができてしまうと、それが何語の辞書であったのかは忘れられてしまった。辞書は自分の腹の中から単語が全部抜けてしまうと、蝉の抜け殻のようになって、翌日から降り始めて止むことのなかった秋雨に濡れて飴のように溶表紙 cover, binding.

3. 心を騒がせる to disturb the heart. 興奮を引き起こす to provoke excitement or agitation. 退屈しきった大使たち ambassadors bored to death; play on *tai-* and *ta*-sounds. 陶酔状態 state of intoxication; rapture. 職業柄 due to the nature of the profession. *The narrator justifies having abruptly mentioned "ambassadors bored to death" by claiming that ambassadors are prone to boredom due to the nature of the profession; humor characteristic of Tawada's writing*. そんなところがまた辞書の村らしいところだ that is also what makes a dictionary village worthy of its name; that is yet another idiosyncracy of a dictionary village. *The logic continues to be humorous: the narrator is alerted to the contradition of ambassadors living in a village, justifies it first by saying that they are indeed found in a dictionary village, then makes it doubly sure by adding, as if by afterthought, that that is why a dictionary village is a dictionary village.*

4. 性格 nature, characteristics. 穏やかな calm, mild, serene. 牛乳 milk. ビールジョッキ a beer tankard. 喉を鳴らして飲む to drink noisily with enjoyment, to gulp down. たまたま＋a verb＝to happen to ～. 糞尿 excrement. Beer may have become smelly because the word "beer" happened to be just under (or above) the word "excrement" in the dictionary. *In Japanese dictionaries, フ-words like ビール are followed by フ-words like 糞尿.* 表面 surface. 泡がたつ to become foamy, bubble. 中性洗剤 a neutral detergent. 垂れ流し effluent; waste outflow. 汚染される to be polluted, contaminated. 色素 pigmentation; coloring. 少なくとも at least. 否定する to deny; reject. 暮らす to live; dwell. This family rejects colors, as a way of life. 徹底する to be thorough, exhaustive; to make something sink in. 俺 I (colloquial masculine first-person). 母乳 breast milk. 苦い bitter. 叔父 uncle. 得意そうに proudly; triumphantly. 不調 disorder; failure; rupture. 災害 disaster; calamity. 口から漏れる to fall from one's lips. 居心地の悪い uncomfortable. 雰囲気 atmosphere. 咳 cough.

けてしまった。表紙のない辞書などというものは窓の無い空と同じで、一度溶けてしまえば歴史に残ることもなく忘れられてしまう。

三 この村には心を騒がせる事件は起こらなかった。だから、たとえば教会の鐘のような大きな音だけが興奮を引き起こし、うまくいけば、退屈しきった大使たちを陶酔状態まで持って行ってくれるかもしれなかった。大使たちは職業柄、退屈しやすい。大使は町に住むのが当然で、村に住んでいるはずがない。しかし辞書の村には確かに大使がいる。そんなところがまた辞書の村らしいところだ。

四 村の人間たちの性格は穏やかである。家の庭にテーブルを置いて、家族が集まって牛乳を飲んでいる。大型のビールジョッキで、喉を鳴らして飲んでいる。ビールのような臭い飲み物は好まれない。ビールという単語がたまたま糞尿という単語の隣にあったため臭くなってしまったのかもしれない。牛乳の表面には泡がたっていて、それは中性洗剤の垂れ流しで汚染された川を思い出させる。テーブルクロスは真っ白だ。お父さんの目の玉も白いし、お兄さんの耳も真っ白。この家族は色素を否定して暮らしている。少なくとも以前はそれが徹底していた。俺の飲んだ母乳は、草の緑色をしていて苦かった、と叔父が得意そうに話し始める。あの頃は、何もかも白かったわけではないのさ。いろいろな自然の不調があって、災害もあって、色が出たりしたものさ。辞書の村では、自然と言う言葉が誰かの口から漏れると、なんだか居心地の悪い雰囲気が広がり、必ず誰かが咳をする。

5. **地面** the land; the earth's surface. **生える** to sprout; grow. **枯れる** to wither. **精たち** spirits; ghosts. **〜に宿る** to stay at 〜; to lodge 〜. **赤子** baby. **〜と共通する** to have in common with 〜; to share. **特徴** peculiarity; feature. **感情** feelings; emotions. **アルカリ性に片寄りがちになった** began to tend to be alkaline. **片寄る／偏る(かたよる)** to incline toward something. **〜がち** to tend, be apt or liable to (do). **嫉妬** envy, jealousy. *In English, green eyes are traditionally associated with jealousy.* **借金** loans; debts, liabilities. **〜に もつれる（縺れる）** to tangle with〜. **ふりほどく** to break free, get loose. **〜に からまる（絡まる）** to twine round 〜; become entangled with〜. Green tangling with green, the more [the villagers] tried to break free the more they became entwined. **攻撃** an attack; assault. **〜に立ち向かう** to face, confront. **ビタミン** vitamin. **葉緑素** chlorophyll. **自己満足** self-satisfaction, complacency. **呼び起こす** to arouse, summon up. **深刻な** grave, serious. **鞄** briefcase; bag. **平気な** calm, unconcerned. **齧る** to chew. **〜に耳を傾ける** to lend an ear to 〜. **日和見主義者** opportunist, fence sitter. **製造される** to be manufactured / produced. **洗濯機** washing machine. **収穫される** to be harvested. **葡萄** grapes. **例外なく** without exception. **抵抗する** to resist. **表題** title. **航海日誌** ship's log. **色女** belle; coquette; concubine; courtesan. **りす（栗鼠）** squirrel. **赤坂** Akasaka ("Red Slope"), a Tokyo neighborhood. **緑が丘** Midorigaoka ("Green Hill"), also a Tokyo neighborhood; -gaoka, or -hill, is a common suffix for place names. **殺人** murderer, murder. **事件** incident, case. **中小企業** small and medium sized businesses. **緑営化** bringing [small and medium sized businesses] under green management. 緑営 (*Ch.* Luying) refers to the Qing Dynasty's green-flagged official army.

6. **機嫌がいい** to be in a good mood, cheerful. **種** seed; topic (of a story); theme; subject. **つきる** to come to an end; run out. **季節** season. **ぱちぱちはじき出される** to be flipped out. Themes of stories are no different from plant seeds; they don't invariably pop in every season.

五　それは、五十年前の雨の降らない夏のことだった。地面に生えていた草がみんな枯れてしまったので、草の精たちは行き場がなくなって、いろいろなところに勝手に宿り始めた。その夏に生まれた赤子たちは、みんな緑の乳を飲んで、性格に共通した特徴が現われた。まず、感情がアルカリ性に片寄りがちになった。これは気をつけないと、巨大な嫉妬や借金を生み出したりする。緑が緑にもつれて、身をふりほどこうとすればするほど、からまってくる。もちろん、そんなことは誰も口に出しては言わないが。他人の攻撃に立ち向かうビタミンは充分あるが、葉緑素が自己満足を呼び起こし過ぎて、深刻な話し合いの最中に急にサンドイッチを鞄から取り出して、平気な顔で齧り始めたりする。人の言うことにはあまり耳を傾けず、そのくせ日和見主義者なのだ。その年は緑の年と呼ばれた。その年に製造された洗濯機で洗うと、白い下着はみんな緑色に変ってしまうのだった。その年に収穫された葡萄で作ったワインは、赤ワインも白ワインも例外なく緑色だった。その年に書かれた本は、作者がどんなに抵抗してみても、表題に〈緑〉という言葉が入ってしまうのだった。緑の航海日誌、緑町の色女、きつね緑とピンクりす、忘れられた緑の太陽、赤坂から緑坂まで、緑が丘殺人事件、中小企業の緑営化。

六　緑の年の話をする時の叔父は機嫌がいい。話の種のつきた時は、みんな叔父に緑の年の話をさせようとする。話の種も植物の種と同じで、どんな季節にも、ぱちぱちはじき出されてくるものではない。

膝ががくがくする to go wobbly at the knees. 喧嘩 argument; fight.沈む to sink; here, to be low in spirits, to feel depressed. アーチ型の背中を持つろば a donkey with an arch-shaped back. 遠洋漁業船のなかで木こりとして働くこと working on a deep-sea fishing boat as a woodsman. 長々と at length, tediously.

7. 去勢される to be castrated; emasculated; neutered. 目覚まし時計 alarm clock. ～を乗り回す to ride around on ～. 静けさを恐れるあまり from excessive fear of the stillness; so afraid of the stillness that [they talk]. 捻り出す to devise (a plan); crank out (a novel). 捻る to twist. 息が詰まる to suffocate. These debates which the father and the uncle squeeze out of their heads because they are so afraid of the stillness are nearly suffocating to the son. 耐え難い difficult to endure. 救う to rescue. 機械 machine, machinery. ドリル drill. 道路工事 road construction. 地表 the surface of the earth.

8. 突き抜ける go through, cut through. 舗装道路 paved streets. 道端 roadside. 握る to grasp. ゆるめる to relax, slacken. 恋愛をして、好かれるにはどうしたらいいのか what to do so as to be in love and be loved in return.

誰も何も言わない季節というものがある。そんな季節には、コーヒーカップも音をたてない。音のない日曜日は恐ろしい。あまりの静けさに膝をがくがくさせながら、叔父が父親と喧嘩を始めるのも、この静けさの中にみんなが沈んでいってしまうのを見るのが怖いからなのだ。アーチ型の背中を持つろばと、遠洋漁業船の中で木こりとして働くこととどちらが寂しいかなどと言う問題について、長々と議論し合うのもそんな時だ。

七 この日、去勢された目覚まし時計が現われた。息子が新しく買ったオートバイにそういう名前を付けて乗り回すことに決めたのだ。静けさを恐れるあまり叔父と父が頭の中から捻り出す議論には息が詰まりそうになる。でも静けさは耐え難い。だから風もないのにカーテンが震えるように踊っているのだろう。静けさから耳を救ってくれるのは機械の音だけだ。これは月曜から土曜まで息子が仕事場で使っているドリルと同じ音を出した。息子は道路工事をしていた。オートバイは、ドリルと同じ音を出しても道に穴を開けることはない。ドリルも本当は穴を開けているわけではない。なぜなら、辞書の国の地表は紙で、その下には何もないからだ。

八 息子は、村を突き抜けて走る舗装道路をオートバイで飛ばしたが、村から遠く離れることはなかった。道端でスカートの縁を風に遊ばせている女性がいても息子はハンドルを握る手をゆるめなかった。恋愛をしたいと思ったが、女性と口をきくのは嫌いだった。恋愛をして、好かれるにはどうしたらい

**尋ねる** to ask. **マッコウクジラ**(抹香鯨) "incense whale," i. e., sperm whale. **脳味噌** brains; brain matter. **香料** perfume. **クジラを殺してしまうくらいならば、恋愛などしなくてもいいくらいクジラが可愛い** 「クジラを殺してしまうくらいならば、恋愛などしなくてもいい」と思うくらいクジラが可愛い; whales were so dear to him that, if being in love meant killing one against his will, he wouldn't want to be in love; he would rather not be in love than kill a whale. **使い捨てる** to use and dispose of; to discard. **そもそも** to begin with, in the first place. **両岸** both banks. **埋め立てる** to reclaim (land) .

9. **裾野** the foot of a mountain. **登山電車** funicular; mountain railway. **警官** police officer. **怪しい** suspicious, mysterious. **観察する** to observe. **朝帰り** returning from an overnight stay at a woman's place or in the pleasure quarters. **犯罪** crime. **虫歯がないだけましだ** if anything, having no bad teeth is an advantage; at least he has no bad teeth. **記号** sign; symbol. **〜を背負う** to be burdened with, to carry. **警官と顔を合わせずに** without [their] eyes meeting the policeman's eyes.

10. **密輸業者** smuggler(s). **下っぱ**(下っ端) underling; gofer; minion. **首の無い人形** a headless doll. *This starts a long explanation of how the underling picked a fight with the suitcase vendor.* **輸入する** to import. **禁じる／られる** to ban / be banned. **船の中で首を縫いつけて，港で税関を通り抜けたら，その首を切り落とせば** if one sews on the head [to the doll] in the boat and then chops it off once having gone through customs. **それでもうりっぱに密輸になるのである** that is good enough to make it an act of smuggling; that is smuggling all right. もう. "already" is emphatic; りっぱに means "fully / sufficiently"; になる to come to a point where it can be assumed or claimed to be. **なると思ったのだ。人生経験の浅い下っぱは** Or so he thought, this underling inexperienced in the ways of the world. **経験の浅い** (*lit.*) shallow in experience.

いのかと、息子は祖母に尋ねた。すると返ってきた答えは、マッコウクジラの脳味噌から取った香料が必要だということ。クジラを殺してしまうくらいならば、恋愛などしなくてもいいくらいクジラが可愛い。だから、クジラが使い捨てた脳を捜しに行かなければならない。でも、クジラはいらなくなった脳味噌をどこに捨てるのだろう。そもそもクジラという単語はどこに住んでいるのだろう。昔ならばクジラは川に住んでいたので、船の中から手を伸ばしてその背中に触ることもできた。今は両岸を埋め立てられて川が狭くなって、クジラは山の中にしか住んでいないので、山に登らなければならない。

九 息子はオートバイに乗って、山の裾野まで走った。それから、山に入るにはまず登山電車に乗るのです、と警官に教えられた。警官は怪しい人間にはみんな親切に道案内をしてやって、そうしながら、その人物をくわしく観察するのだった。ポケットから歯ブラシがのぞいていれば、朝帰りということになるが、それは犯罪ではない。虫歯がないだけましだ。警官の探しているのは、もっと恐ろしい記号を背負った男たちである。そういう男たちは警官と顔を合わせずに電車に乗り込んでしまう。

一〇 密輸業者の下っぱが、登山電車の中で口論していた。首の無い人形を輸入することは禁じられているが、それは船の中で首を縫いつけて、港で税関を通り抜けたら、その首を切り落とせば、それでもう立派に密輸になるのである。なると思ったのだ。人生経験の浅い下っぱは。ところが、縫いつけ

**そう簡単に切り落とせるものではない** [the doll's head] cannot be so easily chopped off [once sewn on]. **折れる** to bend, break. **腫れ上がる** to swell up. **燃え上がる** to flare up, burst into flames. **けらけら笑う** to cackle. **経費** expenditure. **予算を上回る** to go over budget. **従って** accordingly. **儲けが全くないどころか大損をしたところへ** far from making no profit whatsoever, they actually suffered a massive loss, when. . . . **〜に類似したひとつの物** an object that bore a resemblance to 〜. **命令が下った** the order came down [to climb the mountain to find that object]. **何と類似したものなのだ** resemblance to what? **自分で考えろ！** You figure it out! **どなる** to shout; bark; roar. **〜のフライ** fried 〜. **チンピラ** urchins; young hoods; ragamuffins. **むしゃくしゃする** to fret; be irritated; be grumpy. **噛む** to chew. **鞄売り** briefcase salesman. **見物する** to play the spectator. **人の喧嘩を見物するほど楽しいことはない** there is nothing as enjoyable as watching other people argue. **みんなもっと公共の場で喧嘩すればいいのに** it would be great if people fought more often in public. **大道喧嘩屋** street fighters; by analogy with 大道商人 (street vendor), 大道芸人 (street performers), etc. **鼻の頭** the tip of one's nose. **心構え** mental attitude, preparation. If you dab oil taken from a sunflower seed on the tip of your nose and tap your knee lightly three times, you are prepared to fight. **ちょっとでも拍手が起こると、もう嬉しくて** the slightest applause makes you so happy that. **唾** spittle, drool. **染み出す** to run, leak, ooze.

11. **やがて** eventually. **星座をやわらげながら……煙草を吸っている** dimming the constellations, the three sit side by side smoking like delinquent boys seated on a verandah at night. **不良青年** jevenile delinquent; no-goodnik; hoodlum.

てしまえば、人形の首というのはそう簡単に切り落とせるものではない。ハサミは折れるし、指は腫れ上がるし、目は燃え上がる。それを見て人形はけらけら笑う。ボスは怒って、靴を脱いで窓ガラスに投げつける。結局経費は予算を上回って、人形は売れず、従って儲けが全くないどころか大損をしたところへ、山へ登って、〈類似したひとつの物〉を取ってこいという命令が下がった。何と類似したものなのだ、と尋ねても、そんなことは自分で考えろ、とボスはどなるだけ。登山電車の切符は高い。これだけのお金があれば、ポップコーンの入ったスープでもチョコレートのフライでも食べられたのに、と思いながら電車に乗ったチンピラはむしゃくしゃするのでガムを噛んでいるうちに、同じ電車に乗っていた鞄売りの青年と喧嘩になってしまった。人の喧嘩を見物するほど楽しいことはないので、みんなもっと公共の場で喧嘩すればいいのにと思う。そう思う人間はたくさんいるらしい。だからこそ大道喧嘩屋という職業があるのだろう。鼻の頭にひまわりの種から取った脂を塗って、膝を三回軽く打てば、喧嘩の心構えはできる。ちょっとでも拍手が起こると、もう嬉しくて緑色の唾が唇の間から染み出してしまう。しかし登山電車の中にはそんなにたくさん人がいるわけではない。喧嘩するふたりの他には、オートバイから降りて鯨を捜しに行く青年がいるだけだ。

## 二

やがて喧嘩は終わった。星座をやわらげながら、夜の縁側にすわっている不良青年たちのように、三人並んですわって煙草を吸っている。オートバイの青年とチンピラと鞄屋。職業は違っていても、

**首をちょっと傾けるだけで** by merely tilting one's head a little. **死体** corpse. **注射器の針** hypodermic needle. **ひとつきりしかない魂** (*lit.*) the soul that alone exists; the only soul one has. **さすがに目をつむって注射を打つ気にはなれない** after all he cannot bring himself to inject the shot with eyes closed. **砂糖を肉に打ち込めば、家が焼ける** inject sugar into the flesh, and the house will burn; 打ち込めば from 打ち込む, to pound, inject a shot. *A house on fire (火宅) is a Buddhist metaphor for this world of sufferings.* **草の汁を血管に注ぎ込めば、カエルがいっせいに鳴き始める** pour the juice of grass blades into a blood vessel, and frogs will start croaking all at once in unison. *These two lines are reminiscent of the second and third sentences of the opening passage of Natsume Sōseki's* Kusamakura (1906, *Grass Pillow;* tr. The Three-Cornered World, 1965): *"Adhere to principles, and rough edges will form. Punt in an emotional current, and you will be swept away."* **腕立て伏せ** pushups. **歯を食いしばる** to clench or grind one's teeth. **これでは、どうにもならない** at this rate nothing can be done; this is hopeless. **目的地** destination. **恋をするつもりだったっけ** I meant to fall in love, didn't I? **鞄に恋をしてうずくまると、舗装道路にも温もりがある** as he crouched, in love with the bag, he found that even a paved road had warmth. **温もり** warmth. **畔道** a raised footpath between rice fields. **高速道路** an expressway, a highway. **ちょっとあんた、あんたでしょ** Hey, you! It's you, isn't it? あんた is an informal form for あなた. **半端者** an incomplete person, a dullard. **照らされる** to be illuminated. **ぼんやりと** indistinctly, dimly. **ごまかす** to gloss over; fudge; smooth out; also to cheat, deceive, or tamper with]. **身体の右半分がぼんやりとかすんでいて、無いも同様なのだ** the right half of the body is dimly hazed and as good as non-existent. **ある言葉を言いかけて途中でやめた** started to utter a certain word and stopped half way. **この自分も言いかけてやめた言葉のようなものなのだ** he himself is like the word that he left off just as he began to utter it; he himself is something like the word that died on his lips. **そのせいか** perhaps for that reason. **思えてならない** [he] cannot help thinking [that there seems to be no point whatsoever to life, even if he walks about looking for the cast-off grey matter of whales].

喧嘩の後の煙草の味は同じ。彼らの性格は穏やかで、どこから風が吹いてきても、首をちょっと傾けるだけで、死体のにおいは避けることができる。注射器の針の太さを思い浮かべながら、密輸の袋に手を差し入れる。ひとつきりしかない魂を考えると、さすがに目をつむって注射を打つ気にはなれない。砂糖を肉に打ち込めば、家が焼ける。草の汁を血管に注ぎ込めば、カエルがいっせいに鳴き始める。平和の庭で腕立て伏せをしながら、オートバイの青年は歯を食いしばった。これではどうにもならない。どこかに出口があるはずだ。ひとつの道を走り始めても、道そのものが機械や動物でできているから目的地に着くことなどできない。恋をするつもりだったっけ。鞄に恋をしてうずくまると、舗装道路にも温もりがある。月の光が畔道を高速道路にする。ちょっとあんた、あんたでしょ、そう呼びかけられて顔を上げると、半端者の女が月の光に照らされて立っている。半端者というのは、身体の右半分がぼんやりとごまかしたようにかすんでいて、無いも同様なのだ。青年は、ある言葉を言いかけて途中でやめた。自分もやっぱりこうなのだろう、と青年は思った。この自分も言いかけてやめた言葉のようなものなのだ。そのせいか、クジラの捨てた脳味噌を捜して歩いていても、まるで人生に目的がないように思えてならない。

1. 目の前にあるドアは普通一枚だから (*lit.*) because normally the door before my eyes is single, i.e., there is only one door before my eyes.　目覚めという名前の世界に出る then I step out into a world named Awakening.

2. 間違ったドア the wrong door.　取っ手 [door] knob.　「押す」 "Push."　それが、and yet. . . ; ところが.　「とびかかれ」 "Lunge."　あわててとびかかったのがいけなかった what went wrong was that I hastily lunged for the door.　中心から上下ふたつにカクンと折れて breaking across the middle into two pieces.　カクン、バキッ、ボリボリ onomatopoeias conveying the sense, respectively, of breaking, snapping, and crumbling.　あっと言う間に (*lit.*) before you can say "ah!"; in the blink of an eye.　聖書 the Bible.

# Zという町

一 毎朝、眠りのドアを開けて目を覚ます。それが同じひとつのドアなのか、毎日違うドアなのか分からない。目の前にあるドアは普通一枚だから、それを押す。すると、その向こう側にある、目覚めという名前の世界に出る。

二 しかし、その朝わたしは間違ったドアを開けてしまった。いつもならドアの取っ手の隣には「押す」と書いてある。それが、その日は「とびかかれ」と書いてあったので、あわててとびかかったのがいけなかった。しかも、そのドアは、手が触れると、中心から上下ふたつにカクンと折れて、あっと言う間に、それが又左右にバキッと折れて、その四分の一になったドアがまた八分の一にボリボリ、そ

**持っていくべきかどうか迷った** I was of two minds as to whether I should take it with me. **証拠に** for proof. **間違えたドア** the door that I mistakenly used; the wrong door.

3. **目覚めることによって、Zという名前のこの町に来てしまったのだから** because I found myself in this town called Z by waking [not by dreaming]. *Depending on how it is pronounced in Japanese (ゼー, ゼット, or, German style, ツェット) the letter Z for Zürich interestingly alliterates with the German* sehnen *(to long for) or* Sehnsucht *(longing).* **強制的に** forcefully. **憧れ** longing, yearning; originally meaning "wandering away from one's proper place out of longing for someone, somewhere, or something else"—from literary Japanese *aku* (proper place where one belongs) and *karu* (to leave). **自分でも十分承知している** I know well enough myself (that I have found myself in Z because Z is what symbolizes my longing).

4. **Zにいないと何かが欠けているという感じもない** I don't have the sense that unless I am in Z something is missing; it's not that I need to be in Z to feel complete. **憧れというのは、焦がれの一種で** longing is a kind of burning. *A characteristic play on あこがれ／こがれ. The noun form こがれ is rare; the verb こがれる is more common, especially in the compounds 待ちこがれる、恋いこがれる、焦がれ死ぬ.* **肌が沸騰して、ぶつぶつ言って、それで焦げてしまう** the skin boils, simmers, and eventually singes. ぶっぷっ with the pitch accent on the first syllable is an onomatopoeia for simmering and grumbling; ぶつぶつ with the low-pitch first syllable means eruptions on the skin. **実態** substance. **取り敢えず** (*lit.*) without the leisure to bring along what one should; for the moment. **実体がありそうでないものだから** because (the town) has no substance, although seeming to. ありそうでない, does not exist although seeming to, a fixed expression. **その痛みを〜という希望に翻訳すれば** if I translate that pain into a hope [of wanting to go to a town by the name of Z]. **それなりの満足感** satisfaction in its own way. **どうにか痛みも耐えられる** I can manage to withstand the pain as well.

して、最後には本の大きさになって、わたしの手の中にあった。わたしはその聖書のように分厚くて小さい本を持っていくべきかどうか迷った。結局、証拠に持って行くことにした。これがなければ誰も、わたしが眠りの中から間違えたドアを開けたために、Ｚという町に出てしまったのだと話しても信じてくれないだろうから。

三　それが夢であると言うのならば、目を覚ませば自分の町にもどることができる。しかし、わたしは目覚めることによって、Ｚという名前のこの町に来てしまったのだから、どうすればＺを出ることができるのか分からない。しかも、わたしは強制的にここに連れて来られてしまったわけではなく、わたしの憧れを象徴しているのがＺだからＺに来てしまったのだということは、自分でも充分承知している。

四　憧れていると言っても、別にＺにある何かが特に見たいというわけではないし、Ｚにいないと何かが欠けているという感じもしない。憧れというのは、焦がれの一種で、それはただ、肌が沸騰して、ぶつぶつ言って、それで焦げてしまうという感じなのだ。その感じには、名前もないし、実体もない。取り敢えず、その憧れというものにわたしがＺという町の名前を付けたのは、それは町というものも、実体がありそうでないものだから、というだけの話だった。焼けて焦げる時に、その痛みを、Ｚという名前の町に行きたい、という希望に翻訳すれば、どうにか痛みも耐えられる。町に着いた時には、

**中央駅** the Central Station; here Zürich's Hauptbahnhof (Main Station). **麻薬常習犯** chronic drug addict; incurable dope fiend. **と言うように** as if saying. *Note the sentence structure:*

だから、
so [because I most often arrive at the Central Station when I visit Z],
普通は、although usually
駅というのは落ち着かない場所で、a station is a restless place,
麻薬常習犯が捨てた注射の針が脚の裏側に刺さらないかと心配しながら、なるべく足早に通りすぎたい場所なのだけれども、
one that I wish to pass by quickly while worrying that an injection needle a chronic drug addict discarded might pierce the sole of my foot,
Z駅の場合は、in the case of Z station,
さあ欲望を満たせる場所へ到着しましたよ、というように、
じっくり迎え入れてくれる
it welcomes me without haste, as if saying, now, you've arrived at a place where you can fulfill your desire.

**墓に埋められてからも** even after being buried. **それを気にして死人が墓から出て来たりしないように、棺桶にハサミを入れておく** to put scissors in a coffin in advance, so that the dead will not worry about it [having to trim their nails and hair] and come wandering out of their graves. **自分の肌への執着** attachment to one's own skin. **入っていくところを思い浮かべただけで** simply by imagining how (a letter, folded in half, then into four) enters (into a package called an envelope). **じっとしていられない** to be unable to stay still.

5. **自分の憧れの中に彷徨い込んでしまったわたしは** having strayed into the midst of my own longing. **皮膚感覚にさらされている** I am exposed to, or immersed in, a skin sensation [that makes me feel that I exist nowhere]. **一つの町である振りをしているのに騙されて** deceived by [my own desire] that has taken the form of, or is in the guise of, a town.

それなりの満足感もある。着くのは大抵、中央駅だ。だから、普通は、駅というのは落ち着かない場所で、麻薬常習犯が捨てた注射の針が足の裏側に刺さらないかと心配しながら、なるべく足早に通り過ぎたい場所なのだけれども、Ｚ駅の場合は、さあ欲望を満たせる場所へ到着しましたよ、と言うように、じっくり迎えいれてくれる。駅には、床屋もシャワー室も郵便局も喫茶店も本屋もある。だから、髪の毛を切ることもできる。爪や髪の毛が伸びた時にそれを切りたいという欲望ほど強いものはない。墓に埋められてからも爪や髪は伸びるが、それを気にして死人が墓から出て来たりしないように、棺桶にハサミを入れておくのはそのためである。爪や髪を切りたいという気持ちがなくなったら、自分の肌への執着も薄れる。駅には、郵便局もある。手紙を出したいという欲望も強いもので、わたしは手紙がふたつ折りにされて、それから四つ折りにされて、封筒という袋の中に入っていくところを思い浮かべただけで、もうじっとしていられなくなり、手紙を書くことがよくあった。そして、その封筒には、Ｚという町の名前だけが書かれている。人の名前も番号もない。手紙は、憧れであるＺそのものに直接送られていく。

五

しかし、自分の憧れの中に彷徨い込んでしまったわたしは、自分がどこにも存在しないような皮膚感覚にさらされている。なにしろ、わたしが行ってみたいと思っていたある特定の町に到着したわけではなく、わたしの「行きたい」という気持ちそのものが、ひとつの町である振りをしているのに騙

「行ってみたい」というからには as long as [someone] says "I feel like going there." 旅支度をした equipped for a trip.

6. 紙幣 paper bill. オブラート from Dutch *oblaat,* medicinal wafer, also used for candy. 言葉を吐き出す to spew / snap out words. お札 paper bill. 一枚また一枚と one bill after another. 剥がす to peel. 興奮している to be excited. 見たこともないどこかの国のお札 bills of a country somewhere I have never seen. もしかしたらもう存在しない国のもの those of a country which may no longer exist. 苦もなく without effort. 黒い石が金の飾りをまとった巨大な寺院 a colossal cathedral of black stones draped with gold ornaments. 大理石 marble. 宗教 religion. 街路樹 trees lining a street. 路面電車 surface car; streetcar.

7. それが憧れの町だというだけで simply because it is the longed-for town.

されて、その中に迷い込んでしまったのだから。「行ってみたい」と言うからには、旅仕度をした人間がいなければいけないのに、わたしという人間はもういない。

[六] 憧れに向かって、百も千もの言葉を吐き出したいと思っても、言葉は出てこない。そんな時に、紙幣がオブラートのように壁や床に張り付いていることに気がついた。お札があまり薄いので、みんな気がつかないらしい。わたしは、それを一枚また一枚と剥がし始める。一枚剥がすと、その隣にもまだある。それを剥がすと更にもっとたくさん見えてくる。剥がしたお札は全部わたしのものなのだ。わたしは興奮している。そのお金は見たこともないどこかの国のお札で、もしかしたらもう存在しない国のものかもしれず、そうだとしたら使えないのだが、わたしはもともとそれを使うつもりなどない。ただ、お札がいくらでもあって、それをこのように自分だけが苦もなく集めていくことができるということが、たまらなく愉快なのだ。見上げると、それは黒い石が金の飾りをまとった巨大な寺院で、ネクタイをしめた男たちが働いている。彼等のワイシャツは、大理石でできている。これは宗教なのだ、と思うと、お札を剥がして集めるのがつまらなくなった。気がつくと、わたしは街路樹の下のベンチにすわって、路面電車の通り過ぎて行くのを眺めているのだった。

[七] Zでは、それが憧れの町というだけで、どの通りの名前も意味のあるものに思えてくる。通りの名前は便利だからつけられているのだとは思わない。通りの名前などなくても、人は友達の家を見つけ

**郵便配達人** mailman.　**通りの名前が何のためにあるのかは分からないけれども** though I don't know what street names exist for.　**そこを歩く人の気持ちを二重（にじゅう、ふたえ）にする** they [street names] make the feeling of a person walking along the streets double-layered.　**ライオン通り** Löwenstrasse (Lion Street), which stretches southward from Zürich's main station.　**空腹でないときには鹿を襲わない** (lions) do not attack deer unless they are hungry.　**雌** female animal.　**餌** bait, feed.　**雄** male animal.　**思い出さずにいることができない** I cannot help but recall.　**自分の歩いている道に、必ず名称が配給されているということに** [I find a sense of security] in that a name is invariably attributed to each street I walk along.　**親しみ** intimacy, friendliness.　**それを覚えていけば** if I learn them [street names] as I walk along.　**憧れの中を溺れずに泳ぐ技術** (I feel as if I can pick up) the skill of swimming, without drowning, in the midst of Longing.　**道順** route; the way to get to a certain place.　**道に迷う** to lose one's way.　**Zに浸る時間** the time I am immersed in Z.　**その方がいい、とさえ思う** I even think it [getting lost] better.

8. **そういう駅で、通りの名前を使って作ったのは** [a poem] I composed at a station like this, using the names of streets.　**守ってくれようとした** tried to protect me; a reference to Schützengasse ("Protection Alley").　**ウラニア** Urania; a reference to Uraniastrasse.　**星座の詩神** the Muse of the Constellation, a reference to both Uraniastrasse and Urania Observatory on that street. In Greek mythology, Urania is one of the nine Muses and patron of astronomy. Urania was also used as another name for Aphrodite.　**走って行こうか** shall I run?; a reference to Rennweg ("Runway").　**ペリカン** pelican, a reference to Pelikan-strasse and possibly to Fortweg (Fort Road) by which a small Roman fort remains in a garden called Lindenhof (*Fort*=fort, but *fort*=off, away).　**将官** general (army) or flag officer (navy); a reference to General-Guisan-Quai and Gemneral-Wille-Strasse that runs into it. The station street ends in General-Guisan-Quai at the northern end of the lake (Quai=quay).　**財布** purse; a reference to Börsenstrasse (Börse=purse; stock exchange].　**真っ青** pale; a reference to Bleicherweg (Pale Road).　**湖** lake; here, Züricher See (Lake Zürich). *The heavily punctuated style of this song, made up of many street names, is reminiscent of the deliberately verbal translation approach Tawada uses in her* Moji ishoku *(Transplanted Letters, 1999), first published under the title,* Arufabetto no kizuguchi *(Open Wounds in the Alphabet, 1993).*

ることはできるし、郵便配達人は手紙を配達してくれるだろう。通りの名前が何のためにあるのかは分からないけれども、とにかくそこを歩く人の気持ちを二重にする。ライオン通りを歩いていると、ライオンとは何の関係もないわたしは、ライオンは空腹でない時には鹿を襲わないとか、雌が餌を捕ってくる間、雄は昼寝をしているとか、そういう話を思い出さずにいることができない。自分もそうだろうか、自分は違うだろうか、とライオンと自分を比べる。自分の歩いている道に、必ず名称が配給されているということに、わたしは安心感を覚える。わたしは、文字というものに何よりも親しみを覚える。しかもそれは、憧れという町の通りの名前ばかりであるから、それを覚えていけば、憧れの中を溺れずに泳ぐ技術が身に付くような気がする。わたしには道順というものがなかなか覚えられない。道に迷うことなど、別に怖いとも思わない。むしろ、道に迷えば迷うほど、Zに浸る時間は長くなるわけだから、その方がいい、とさえ思う。

八　ところで、わたしがそういう駅で、通りの名前を使って作ったのは、次のような歌だった。「町は、守ってくれようとした、父親ライオンのように、でも、わたしの探すのは女神ウラニア、星座の詩神、走って行こうか、ペリカンが飛び立つ前に、ああもう遅い、将官が財布を閉めて、真っ青になって、それから、湖に飛び込んだ」。

九　歌を忘れれば、道は分からなくなる。歌を忘れても、甘いものを食べれば記憶はもどるのだと言う

9. 包み紙に包まれて wrapped in wrapping paper.　停留所 bus or streetcar stop. もう前歯の跡をつけてしまっていた I had already left the imprint of my front teeth.　罪 crime.　非難する to criticize; blame; reproach.　堂々と振る舞うしかない I have no choice but to behave in an assertive manner.　セロハン cellophane.　リボン ribbon.　光を反射して奇麗で、急に涙が出そうになった [cellophane wraps and ribbons] reflected the lights and looked so beautiful that I was suddently on the verge of tears.　銀色の包み紙を恥じる様子もなくむしって tearing off the silver paper wrap with no sign of shyness.　常識に反すること what goes against common sense.　わざと大きめの声で in a deliberately louder voice.　それが反転することなく without becoming reversed [from faintly salty to sweet].　発言する to speak up; make a statement.

10. 憧れで咽喉が詰まって chock-full of longing; choking from too much longing.

人もいる。わたしの持っていた聖書のような本はいつの間にか消えていた。消えたと思ったら、包み紙に包まれて、路面電車の停留所のベンチの上にあった。聖書が入っているのだろうと思って、包み紙を破いて開くと、それはホワイトチョコレートだった。わたしは、いつの間にか店の中に立っていて、まだ料金を払っていないチョコレートを裸にして、もう前歯の跡を付けてしまっていた。恥ずかしいけれどもそこで赤くなったら、みんなわたしの罪に気がついて、非難し始めるだろう。わたしは、少しも恥ずかしいことなどしていない人のように、堂々と振る舞うしかない。そうだ、わたしは、憧れの中にいるのだから、やってみたいことは何でもやっていいんだ。店の中は、菓子を包むセロハンやリボンが光を反射して奇麗で、急に涙が出そうになった。客たちはわたしが店の中で、銀色の包み紙を恥じる様子もなくむしって、平気でホワイトチョコレートを食べているので、あきれて言葉をさがしていた。みんなの常識に反することをすると、途端にみんなの目に見えてしまうらしい。そこで、わたしは自分には人に隠さなければならないようなことは何もないのだと主張するために、わざと大きめの声で、「チョコレートが甘いというのは間違えで、チョコレートは食べた瞬間、かすかに塩の味がするのに、それが反転することなく、いつの間にか砂糖の味になっているところが面白いです」と発言した。すると、そこにいた人達は、みんな顔を背けて、店を出ていった。

一〇

わたしは、Zにいるというだけで、憧れで喉が詰まって、ものが食べられないような気がしていた塊 lump. 困惑する to be confused; perplexed. 欲しいものを欲しいと思うよりも早く、欲しい気持ちが手の形になって、それを奪ってしまう even before I realize I desire that which I wish to have, my desire takes the form of a hand to wrest the object away. それはだから、わたしの腕ではないのだけれど so it's not my arm [that does the robbing], but. そんなことを言っても聞いてもらえない no one would listen to such an excuse. 「オメガ」 "Ω" or small letter "ω"; "Z," which stands for Zürich in Switzerland, is the last letter of the Roman alphabet, while "Ω," or Omega, which is a Swiss watch brand name, is the last letter in the Greek alphabet. 盗人 thief; somewhat obsolescent but often used with humor. 駅前通り station road; here, Bahnhofstrasse, a famous shopping street, stretches 1.4 kilometers southward from the station all the way to Lake Zürich. 水の表面が広がっている光景 a scene of spreading water surface. それは、自由意志で無理やり来させられた町ではない it is not a town that I have been forced to visit of my own free will. *A deliberately contradictory sentence. The narrator has wished to be in Z of her free will, yet finds herself in Z as if by force.* その町自身がひそかに夢見る水の風景 a water scene that the town itself secretly dreams about.

11. ヨット yacht. 広場 square; plaza; here, Bürkliplatz, a busy quayside connecting General-Guisan-Quai that faces the north edge of the lake and Quai Bridge over Limmat River where it flows out of the lake. 隔てる to separate; interpose. あらゆる方向からやって来た路面電車という思考 thoughts called surface cars coming from all directions. 回路を変更しながら while changing their circuits. 横断する to cross. 車輪たちはわたしをひき殺そうとしている the wheels are about to run over me. あの線が走り去り、この線が来る前ならば、渡れるはず、などと計算してみるのだが、やっぱり渡れない I should be able to cross, I calculate, if I do so after a streetcar has sped past on that line and before another comes on this line, but I still cannot cross. レミ通り Rämistrasse, which hits the northeast end of the lake and leads into the Quay bridge.

のに、そのように大きなチョコレートの塊を手に入れてしまったので困惑していた。欲しいものを欲しいと思うよりも早く、欲しい気持ちが手の形になって、それを奪ってしまう。それはだから、わたしの腕ではないのだけれど、そんなことを言っても聞いてもらえない。それから、わたしは腕時計を手にしていた。時刻が知りたかったのではない。この町では、時間は先へ進まないので、時刻なんてどうでもいい。時計を盗んでしまったのは、ショーウインドウにギリシャ語アルファベットの最後の文字「オメガ」が書いてあったからだ。Zもアルファベットの最後の文字だけれども、ギリシャ語の最後の文字というのが、どうしても欲しくなってしまった。わたしは盗人として、駅前通りを歩いていくことになった。わたしは水のある方向へ歩いて行けば、それで救われるのだろうと思った。水の表面が広がっている光景、それはもう町ではない。それは、自由意志で無理やり来させられた町ではない。その町自身がひそかに夢見る水の風景だ。

二

　ヨットのマストが見える。わたしはすぐそこにある湖に行き着くことができない。広場が、わたしと水を隔てている。あらゆる方向からやってきた路面電車という思考が回路を変更しながら走っていく、その広場をわたしは横断することができない。車輪たちはわたしを轢き殺そうとしている。あの線が走り去り、この線が来る前ならば、渡れるはず、などと計算してみるのだが、やっぱり渡れない。何度も最初の一歩を踏み出してみたが、それ以上、先に進むことができない。そこを渡れば、レミ通

**管** tube; pipe.

12. **右手に現れるだろうリマト川** the Limmat River that should appear on the right; the river flows from Lake Zürich and through the city, one or two blocks to the east from the station road. **意地悪** nasty. **よじれ、とぎれ、とける** [the topography] twists, comes to an end, and melts away. *A characteristic play on the sounds of the words.* **これは夢でさえなく、わたしは目が覚めてしまっているのだった** this was not even a dream for I had woken from it.

13. **呼吸** breathing. **それどころか** far from that; much more than that. *Watch the structure of the long sentence starting with this:*

この焦げる痛さに反応して足を動かしているだけで
I am merely moving my legs in response to this burning pain;
Zでは何も探していないし、I am not looking for anything in Z
このように町に包まれて幸福だと繰り返し自分に言って聞かせるのは
the reason I tell myself repeatedly I am happy to be enveloped by a town like this
実は自分が 町を壊したい、と思っているのを認めるのが怖いからなのだ is in fact because I am afraid of admitting that I wish to destroy the town,
というようなことが分かってきてしまった such were the thoughts that had already dawned on me.

**星が汗のように現れても** even if [the sun begins to set and] stars emerge like [drops of] perspiration. *This is an unconventional expression not idiomatic in Japanese.* **ぎゃくに、Zを壊してしまえば、わたしをうごかすエネルギーの源が絶えてしまうから、歩けなくなってしまうかもしれない** Conversely, if I destroy Z, the source of energy that moves me will come to an end and I may no longer be able to walk. **覚醒** awakening. **救う** to rescue; save; deliver; release. Will another awakening help me out [of this dilemma]?

りの入り口に入ることができ、後はその管をぐっと上り詰めれば、それで満足できるのだ、と想像してみる。

一二　渡れないのならば仕方ない。諦めて、別の道を探そう。この通りを戻って、それから右手に現われるだろうリマト川を渡って、道があってもなくても、坂を上がって行こう、と決心した。しかし、夢の地形は意地悪で、よじれ、とぎれ、とける。しかも、これは夢でさえなく、わたしは目が覚めてしまっているのだった。

一三　坂を上り始めれば、呼吸が早くなるから、物の考え方も変ってくる。わたしはＺがあってもなくても関係ない、という気になってくる。それどころか、わたしはこの焦げる痛さに反応して足を動かしているだけで、Ｚでは何も探していないし、このように町に包まれて幸福だ、と繰り返し自分に言ってきかせるのは、実は自分が町を壊したい、と思っているのを認めるのが怖いからなのだ、というようなことが分かってきてしまった。Ｚを破壊したい。Ｚを壊さなければ、日が暮れて星が汗のように現われても、いつまでもその中を歩き回っていなければならない。逆に、Ｚを壊してしまえば、わたしを動かすエネルギーの源が絶えてしまうから、歩けなくなってしまうかもしれない。

それとも、その時には、また別の覚醒がわたしを救ってくれるのだろうか。

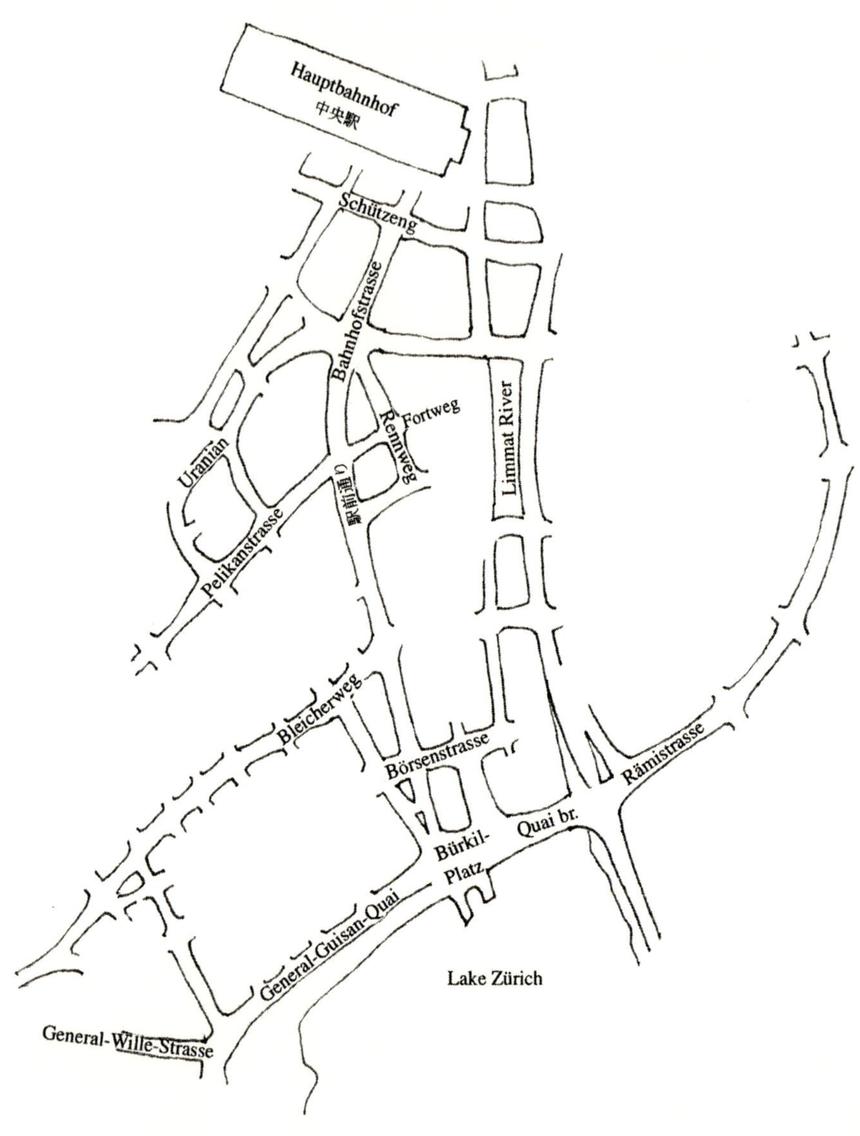


Zürich between the Central Station (Hauptbahnhof) and Lake Zürich

# 友よ

林　京子

# My Friend

*Hayashi Kyōko*

HAYASHI KYŌKO was born in Nagasaki in 1930, but she spent much of her prewar and wartime childhood in Shanghai. Returning to Nagasaki in March 1945, five months before the war ended, she attended Nagasaki Girls High School. She was working at a munitions plant in Nagasaki when the atomic bomb was dropped on August 9. She was seriously ill for two months, and like the majority of bomb survivors, suffered thereafter from fragile health and fear of passing on radiation-related illness to her child. She started to write in 1962.

Hayashi made her literary debut with the Akutagawa Prize-winning "Matsuri no ba" (1975, tr. "Ritual of Death"), which records her exodus from the area of devastation and eventual reunion with her family. Hayashi continued to write of the atomic bomb in a short story "Nanjamonja no men" (Masks of Whatchamacallit, *Gunzō*, February 1976), and a sequence of twelve short stories called *Giyaman bīdoro* (Cut Glass, Blown Glass, 1978). The fifth story "Kōsa" (tr. "Yellow Sand"), dealing with the author's wartime experience in Shanghai, has a special place in the sequence.

*Missheru no kuchibeni* (Michelle's Lipstick, 1980) is a fuller account of her girlhood in Shanghai. *Shanghai* (1985 winner of the Women's Literature Prize) is a travelogue based on a five-day trip to the city thirty-six years after she had last seen it.

In *Naki ga gotoshi* (As If Nothing Had Happened, 1981), her first full-length novel, Hayashi alludes to her determination to be Nagasaki's "chronicler." Her effort as a chronicler in the sixties and seventies led her to recount the bombing, to explore the psychology of survivors, and to write of the fate of her friends and teachers. In the eighties her topics became more diverse: marriage, birth, divorce, her grown son's marriage, the birth of his children, the environment, aging, and death, all nevertheless intricately connected to the bombing and war. Some stories in *Michi* (The Road, 1985) concern the narrator's son who is a *hibaku nisei* (second generation victim of the bomb), and her divorced husband. *Sangai no ie* (No Abode, 1985), whose title story won the 1983 Kawabata Prize, adds depth to Hayashi's study of human psychology through the theme of her father's death and the relationship between her parents. Stories in *Tanima* (The Valley, 1988) and *Vājinia no aoi sora* (The Blue Skies of Virginia, 1988) draw on her experiences during three years of residence near

Washington D.C. *Yasurakani ima wa nemuritamae* (Rest Now in Peace, 1990) is a requiem for a teacher whose journal documenting the lives of war-mobilized girl students was found thirty years after her death. In *Seishun* (Youth, 1994), a novel about a group called Chūgoku Kenkyūkai (China Study Group), Hayashi wrote for the first time of her postwar youth.

*Nagai jikan wo kaketa ningen no keiken* (Human Experiences over Long Time, 2000) won the Noma Literary Prize. The title novella concerns her pilgrimage to the thirty-three temples on the peninsula where she lives. The other piece, "From Trinity to Trinity," is a record of her trip to Los Alamos, New Mexico, the site of the first atomic bomb test, i.e, the source of her fifty-five years of experience. Both journeys were undertaken in an effort to sort out, before the end of the century, her August 9th experiences and reflections. The pilgrimage fulfilled the promise she had made to a missing Nagasaki friend that they would be co-pilgrims, while the visit to the Trinity Site was made so that "what started at Trinity should end at Trinity."

The piece selected for this volume "Tomo yo," concerns a reunion with a classmate after thirty years, and the discovery that the friend's stories had remained untold all that time. Thinking that she and her friend shared similar feelings as fellow victims of the bombing, the narrator finds that her assumptions were flawed, and that their experiences were incommensurable, after all.

## WORKS IN ENGLISH TRANSLATION

"Ritual of Death" (Matsuri no ba). Kyoko Selden, tr. In *Nuke-Rebuke: Writers and Artists against Nuclear Energy and Weapons,* Morty Sklar, ed. The Spirit That Moves Us Press, 1984.

"Yellow Sand" (Kōsa). Kyoko Selden, tr. In *Japanese Women Writers*, translated and edited by Noriko Mizuta Lippit and Kyoko Iriye Selden. M.E. Sharpe, 1991.

"Empty Can" (Akikan). Margaret Mitsutani, tr. In *Atomic Aftermath: Short Stories about Hiroshima and Nagasaki,* edited by Ōe Kenzaburō. Shūeisha, 1984.

"Two Gravemarkers" (Futari no bohyō). Kyoko Selden, tr. In *The Atomic Bomb: Voices from Hiroshima and Nagasaki*, edited by Kyoko and Mark Selden, M. E. Sharpe, 1989.

"My Friend" (Tomo yo). Kyoko Selden, tr. In *Review of Japanese Culture and Society*, Center for Inter-Cultural Studies and Education, Jōsai University, December 1999-2000 (double issue).

"Masks of Whatchamacallit" (Nanjamonja no men). Kyoko Selden, tr. In *Review of Japanese Culture and Society*, December 2004.

1. なしてか、この日は暑かとさ somehow, this day [August 9th] is always hot each year—the mother's speech is in Nagasaki dialect. In standard Japanese this would be なぜか、この日はあついのよ. 光が溜まるのだろうか perhaps light collects. ～に暑さがささる shafts of heat pierce [our shoulders and lower legs]; *暑さ and ささる form an unusual combination, deliberately used to suggest shards of glass piercing the skin.*

2. 記憶にある限り as long as she [the mother] remembers. まっ盛り peak. 私が受けた閃光の暑さ the heat of the flash I experienced; a reference to the Nagasaki A-bomb on August 9, 1945.

3. 被爆する to be bombed. *This expression is used only in relation to Hiroshima and Nagasaki. Cf. 被曝, exposure to radiation.* 長崎を離れて生活をするようになってから after I came to lead my life away from Nagasaki.

# 友よ

一 なしてか、この日は暑かとさ、と坂の下まで見送ってきた母が言った。坂の下には、光が溜るのだろうか。立っていると素肌の肩や足に、暑さがささってくる。

二 母が長崎市内に住むようになってから、二十七年が過ぎている。二十七回迎えた八月九日は、記憶にある限り、いつでも暑い、という。夏のまっ盛りだから、暑いのがあたりまえだが、母の八月九日にも、私が受けた閃光の熱さが重なってくるのだろう。

三 だけど、いい気持ちよ、と空車を探しながら私は言った。被爆してから三十二年間に、私が長崎で迎える八月九日は、これで二回目である。学生時代の夏休みにも、長崎を離れて生活をするようになっ

**八月の長崎に足を踏み入れることを** setting foot in Nagasaki in August. **意識してさけてきた** I have consciously avoided [setting foot in Nagasaki in August]. **まともに日をあびてみると** as I now bathed in direct light. **いくら熱く照りつけていても** no matter how hard [the sun] beat down on me. **自然の光** natural light, as opposed to the flash of the atomic bomb.

4. **傘か帽子はいらんと** 傘か帽子はいらないの？ in standard dialect. **リボンがついたピケ帽** a pique hat with a ribbon around it, with ribbon ends hanging in back. **ばってん** (*Nagasaki dialect*) but, even so; explained in Yamazaki Yoshishige's *Seji hyakudan* (Sundry Episodes on Worldly Matters, 1843) as a dialectal form of ばとて (though one might say so), the expression is interestingly similar in sound and meaning to the English "but then." ばってん would be でも or けれど in standard dialect. **式はなんかよ、校庭であっとやろ** 式はながいわよ、校庭であるのでしょう？ The ceremony is long; it's going to be held in the schoolyard, yes? なんか (*Nagasaki dialect*) corresponds to ながい in standard dialect. **覚えとるね** you remember (what your friend Nakada looks like), yes? 覚えているの or 覚えているよね in standard Japanese. **N 高女** N[agasaki] Girls High School. **三十三回忌たいね** [today] would have been the thirty-third anniversary of your death. たいね in Nagasaki dialect corresponds to だね or だよね in standard dialect. *The thirty-third anniversary, an important anniversary along with the third, seventh, and thirteenth, occurs thirty-two years after death, because the year of death counts as the first. This sets the date of the story at 1977.*

5. **正門** front gate. **原爆死亡者の追悼式典** commemoration of the A-bomb dead. **お悔やみを言う** to offer condolences.

てからも、八月の長崎に足を踏み入れることを、私は意識して避けてきた。長崎の、明るすぎる夏の光が、私は怖かったのである。しかし、こうして、まともに光をあびてみると、太陽がいくら暑く照りつけていても、自然の光は柔らかく、心地がよかった。

[四]傘か帽子はいらんと、と母が、玄関を出るときから言っている同じ言葉を、繰り返して言った。リボンがついたピケ帽？と私は笑って言った。私たち姉妹が小学生のころ、夏になると母は必ず、可愛らしくみえるから、と言って、白いピケ帽をかぶせた。パブリックスクールの西洋人の子供たちがピケの帽子をかぶっているのをみて、母は、同じ帽子を娘たちにもかぶせてみたかったらしい。母も思い出して、ばってん、式はなんかよ、校庭であっとやろ、と笑って言った。それから、中田さんていう人の顔は覚えとるね、と聞いた。中田和子とは、N高女を卒業してから、はじめて逢うのである。三十年ぶりになる。

あんたが死んどれば、今日は三十三回忌たいね、と母が言った。

[五]中田との待ち合せの時間は、八時である。城山小学校の正門に、八時までに着かなければならない。城山小学校で行われる原爆死亡者の追悼式典は、八時十分からはじまる。はじまる前に中田と逢って、お悔やみを言いたい。中田の夫は、一年前に病死している。

6. **まだ二十分はありますもんね** we still have at least 20 minutes. **出勤時間ばってん何とか行けるでしょう** though it's rush hour I think we'll manage [to get there on time].

7. **浦上川沿いの** along the Urakami River. **城山小学校** an elementary school approximately 500 meters from the hypocenter. **爆心地から半径一キロメートル以内** within a one kilometer radius of the hypocenter. **兵器工場** arms factory; a reference to Mitsubishi Arms Factory's Ōhashi Plant to the north of the hypocenter. *The hypocenter is approximately at the midpoint between this plant and Mitsubishi Arms Factory's Morimachi Plant to the south.* **円内からややはずれた一・四キロメートルの地点にあたる** is 1.4 kilometers [from the hypocenter] slightly beyond the circle with a radius of one kilometer.

8. **まあ、むかしになるかしら** well, I suppose it's getting to be long ago. **話には聞きますばってんね** 話には聞きますけれどもね; I have heard of it but [I don't know it personally].

9. **金毘羅山** the name of a mountain to the east of the hypocenter just beyond the circle with a radius of 1.5 kilometer. **市内を縦走する四百メートルたらずの山** a mountain not quite 400 meters high, running through the city. **コンクリートの堰** concrete dam. **たんぼ** rice paddies.

10. **逃げる途中でぬげたのか、堰を渡るときにぬいだのか** whether [my clogs] slipped off on the way there or I took them off when crossing the dam. **水苔** incrustation; bog moss. **流れを止められた水面が盛り上がって、落差がついた川床に、白いしぶきになって散っていた** the water, its surface heaving from being dammed, scattered in white spray onto the riverbed at a lower water level.

六 行き先と待ち合わせの時間を運転手に告げて、私はタクシーに乗った。まだ二十分はありますもんね、出勤時間ばってん何とか行けるでしょう、と運転手が言った。

七 母が住んでいる坂の上の町も、城山小学校がある浦上川沿いの城山の街も、かつての爆心地から半径一キロメートル以内にある。中田や私が被爆した兵器工場は、円内からややはずれた一・四キロメートルの地点にあたるが、城山小学校に行くためには、その前を通るはずだ。兵器工場の前を通りますか、と私は、運転手に聞いてみた。

八 兵器工場って、むかしのですか、と運転手が言った。ええ昔の、と答えてから、私は、まあ、むかしになるかしら、と言いなおした。話には聞きますばってんね、と運転手が言った。戦争が終わってから生まれたらしい運転手は、どの辺りが兵器工場の跡なのか、わからない、と言った。

九 走っているタクシーの左側に、金毘羅山の山並みが見えている。金毘羅山は、あの日に私が逃げて行った山である。長崎市内を縦走する四百メートルたらずの山だが、兵器工場を逃げ出して金毘羅山に行くまでに、私は、巾の広い川を渡った。川には、コンクリートの堰が築いてあった。たんぼに水をひくための堰で、私は、堰の上をはだしで渡った。

一〇 逃げる途中でぬげたのか、堰を渡るときにぬいだのか、私は、片方だけの下駄をさげて、水苔が生えている堰を歩いた。流れを止められた水面が盛り上がって、落差がついた川床に、白いしぶきになっ川の流れまでは変えられないだろう [the changes] would not have gone so far as to affect the course of the river; at least the river course would have remained unaltered. ～で塗り固められた solidly covered with ～.

11. 踏切り railroad crossing. 十字に交わっている [the crossing barrier and our road] intersected at a right angle. 遮断機 the crossing barrier. 一間巾の狭いホーム a narrow platform about two meters wide. *The expression 向かいあった in the last sentence of the paragraph indicates that there were a pair of platforms each about two meters wide.* 巾に見あったトタン板の屋根 zinc roofs of approximately the same width [as the platforms]. ペンキ paint.

12. 市電 streetcar. 諫早に通じている国鉄の汽車 the national railway that connected to Isahaya. *Isayaha, located to the west of Nagasaki, is a center of transportation and economy at the intersection of Nagasaki, Shimabara, and Sonoki peninsulas.* 赤錆びたレール rails that were red with rust. それにしては considering [that this was not a bus line but a railroad]. レールが錆ついている the rails were rusted over; the rails looked too rusty for use by trains.

て散っていたのを、覚えている。街の様子は変わってしまっているが、川の流れまでは変えられないだろう。あのときの川が見つかれば、兵器工場の跡は見当がつく。私は、道の両側に川を探した。川は、見あたらず、コンクリートで塗り固められた道が、光を照り返して真っ直に続いている。坂の多い長崎の街にしては、珍しい直線の道である。

二一 十分ほど走ったところ、道は少しばかり上り坂になった。ゆるい坂を上って、下った坂の下に踏切りがあった。踏切りと、タクシーが走っている道路とは十字に交っている。城山小学校は踏切りをつっ切って五、六分走ったあたりらしいが、この踏切りに、私は見覚えがあった。遮断機が降りている踏切りの際に、一間巾の狭いホームがある。ホームには、巾に見あったトタン板の屋根がついており、緑色のペンキを塗ったベンチが一つ置いてある。向かいあったホームに、出勤するサラリーマンたちが乗物を待っている。

二二 乗物が市電なのかバスなのか、あるいは諫早に通じている国鉄の汽車なのか、私には判断がつかなかった。赤錆びたレールが敷かれているから、バスの路線ではないようだが、それにしてはレールが錆びついている。

二三 ただ、私の記憶が正しいならば、それは市電のホームで、かつて私が学徒のころ、兵器工場に通うために利用していた、大橋の停留所のはずである。そのころは大橋の停留所が終点で、それから先の

13. **学徒** a mobilized student, from 学徒勤労動員 (がくときんろうどういん), the mobilization of students, seventh graders and up, as workers during WW II. *First it was occasional, but it became four months a year in 1943, then all year in 1944, involving over 2 million students.*
**停留所の先が踏み切りになっていて、線路らしき**（*spoken J.* らしい）**ものが延びて行っている** beyond the stop was a railroad crossing and something like a railway stretched ahead. **列をなして** in columns. **停留所の先が踏み切りになっていて** (but now) there was a crossing barrier just beyond the stop, and (something like a railway stretched ahead).

14. **大橋の停留所** the name of the streetcar stop near the Mitsubishi Arms Factory. **よう知っとんなるですね** よく知っておいでですね.

15. **アカサコ**（赤迫）the name of the new terminal; *written in katakana because the narrator did not recognize it.*

16. **昭和二十年** 1945.

17. **腐食する** to corrode. **小さな、針で突いたような無数の穴から光が抜けて……蜂の巣のように揺れ動いている** light sifted through those countless small holes that looked as if they had been made by a needle and fell in a wavering honeycomb of light on the backs of the white shirts of the people below. **自分一人が年を経て、三十二年前の風景を眺めている、奇妙な錯角に襲われた** I was visited by an odd illusion that the years had passed for me alone, and that I was looking at the identical landscape of thirty-two years ago. **真夏の外気から隔絶された、タクシーの冷房のせい** because of the air-conditioning in the taxi, cut off from the outside air of midsummer.

兵器工場までの道を、学徒も工員も、列をなして歩いていた。終点の停留所から工場の正門までは、歩いて十分はかかったが、いま見ると、停留所の先が踏切りになっていて、線路らしきものが延びて行っている。

[一四]　ここは大橋の停留所でしょう、と私は運転手に尋ねてみた。よう知っとんなるですね、と運転手が言った。

[一五]　終点じゃなかった？と私は聞いた。いまはアカサコまで行っとりますよ、と私の知らない土地の名前を、運転手が言った。私は、腕の時計を見た。八時に七、八分前である。

[一六]　昭和二十年の八月九日の、ちょうど同じ時刻ごろ、私はこのホームで市電をおりた。あの日の朝も、今日のようによく晴れていた。

そして今日まで、一度も私はこの場所へきたことがない。

[一七]　ホームの屋根のトタン板が腐蝕して、穴があいている。小さな、針でつついたような無数の穴から光が抜けて、ホームを歩く人たちの頭髪や、白いワイシャツの背中で蜂の巣のように、揺れ動いている。出勤時の風景は、三十二年前の朝と変りがなかった。遮断機が上るのを待っているタクシーの中から、私はホームの風景を眺めていた。私は、自分一人が年を経て、三十二年前の風景を眺めている、奇妙な錯覚に襲われた。真夏の外気から隔絶された、タクシーの冷房のせいだろうか。それとも、思

**思いが切実に重ならない違和感** the sense of malaise, which kept me from keenly identifying with the place.

18. **きっかりに** ちょうどに, exactly. **国民学校** (*lit.*) national school, now 小学校. The Japanese elementary school was called 国民学校 between 1941 and 1947. **分散されて** broken up and dispatched [from the factory]. **即死** instant death.

19. **欠かさずに** without skipping [a year]. **平和公園** Peace Park at the epicenter. **原爆炸裂時刻** the moment of the A-bomb explosion. **黙とう（黙祷）を捧げる** to offer a silent prayer; here, join in silent prayer. **例年のしきたり** annual practice.

20. **全壊した校舎の跡地に建てられた** built at the site of the totally destroyed school building. **五十段はある石段** stone steps, of which there were at least fifty. **指示されたように** as instructed. **中田らしき**（*spoken J.* らしい）**人影は見あたらなかった** found no sign of anyone like Nakada. **石の門柱** stone pillars at the gate.

21. **三年生以上の高学年生** third through sixth graders. 高学年生 (upper class children) usually refers to fifth and sixth graders. **半ズボンや、短いスカートの裾から伸びた足** legs stretching from shorts and skirt hems. **しっかりと肉がしまっていて** taut-muscled.

いが切実に重ならない違和感は、私の中でも八月九日は遠い昔になってしまったせいだろうか。

一八 約束の時間きっかりに、タクシーは城山小学校に着いた。城山小学校は、中田の出身校である。戦時中の卒業生だから、当時の城山国民学校になる。記録によると八月九日の当日、学校には百五十一名の人たちがいた。兵器工場から分散されてきていた学徒や、城山国民学校の教職員たちである。そのうちの百三十一名が死亡している。中田の恩師たちは、殆どが即死している。

一九 中田は、恩師たちの慰霊のために毎年、欠かさずに追悼式に出席していた。小学校での追悼式典が終わると、歩いて二十分ばかりで行ける爆心地の平和公園に行き、十一時二分の、原爆炸裂時刻の黙とうを捧げる。これが中田の例年のしきたりになっている。長崎で生活をしていない私は、今日一日を中田の行動に従うつもりでいた。

二〇 現在の城山小学校は、全壊した校舎の跡地に建てられたものである。小高い丘になっていて、正門までには五十段はある石段を上らなくてはならない。私は、指示されたように石段を上った。中田らしき人影は見あたらなかった。私は、石の門柱のまん前に立って中田を待った。

二一 追悼式に出席する児童たちが、石段を上ってくる。夏休みなので、出席する子供たちは三年生以上の高学年生に限られているようだ。半ズボンや、短いスカートの裾から伸びた足は、しっかりと肉が茶褐色に日焼けしている sun-tanned a dark tea-brown. 海に近いせいか perhaps because [the city] is close to the sea.

22. 立像 statue, standing image. 左の腕に一羽のハト（鳩）を止まらせた with a dove on his left arm. *Botanical and animal names nowadays are often written in katakana.* 児童 schoolchildren. 報道関係の注文に応じて in response to the request of the media. 両手をあわせて with palms joined. 写されるのに慣れていて used to being photographed. 素直に感情を出して without inhibiting their spontaneous feelings.

23. 炎天下の校庭をさけて avoiding the schoolyard in the scorching sun. 喪服を着た in mourning. 白地に黒い線書き模様の、絹地のワンピース a one-piece dress with black line-drawn patterns against a white background. 小刻みに、つま先で駆け上がってくる足の運び具合 the way she ran up in small steps on her toes. 石段を見上げて、誰かを探しているらしい丸い、黒い目の動き the way her round, black eyes moved, apparently looking for someone as she glanced upward along the steps.

24. お互いを確かめあう必要はなかった we had no need to confirm who each other was. 息をはず（弾）ませて her breath bouncing, i.e., somewhat out of breath. 僅かにひきつった twitched / tightened up slightly. ガラス片の傷跡 scar from a piece of glass. *Glass fragments, along with beams and roof tiles blown off collapsing buildings, caused most mechanical injuries.* 知っているものが注意をしてみなければわからないほどに、薄くなっている had become so faint that it was unnoticeable unless someone who knew about it looked carefully.

しまっていて、首筋や肩が、茶褐色に日焼けしている。長崎の街は海に近いせいか、子供たちは夏休みじゅう海に行って遊んでいる。

二二 石段を上りきった校舎の正面に、少年の立像があった。左の腕に一羽のハトを止まらせたブロンズの像は、「少年平和像」と呼ばれて、被爆死した児童たちの供養の像である。四、五人の子供たちが、報道関係のカメラマンの注文に応じて、黄色と白との菊の花束を少年に捧げ、両手を合せて黙とうをしている。毎年のことなのだろう。子供たちは写されるのに慣れていて、カメラの前で、素直に感情を出して祈っている。

二三 ベルが鳴った。追悼式典がはじまる合図のベルである。式は、炎天下の校庭をさけて、講堂で行われるようだ。児童や、喪服を着た大人たちが、別棟になっている講堂に入って行く。ベルの音を聞いて、数人の子供たちが石段を駈け上ってくる。その中に、白地に黒い線描き模様の、絹地のワンピースを着た中年の女がいる。小刻みに、つま先で駈け上ってくる足の運び具合も、石段を見あげて、誰かを探しているらしい丸い、黒い目の動きも、少女のころの中田に似ている。

二四 三十年ぶりの再会でありながら、私たちは、おたがいを確かめあう必要はなかった。待った?と中田が息をはずませて聞いた。左の唇の端の傷が、話しかけるときに、僅かにひきつった。八月九日に受けたガラス片の傷跡は、知っている者が注意をして見なければわからないほどに、薄くなっている。

25. 整列して fallen in; lined up.　遺族席なのか、喪服を着た大人たちが坐っている apparently these chairs were meant for bereaved relatives, since adults in mourning were seated in them.

26. 〜にのぼる amounting to 〜.　奇蹟的に miraculously.

27. 椅子が置いてある場所をさけて avoiding the area where chairs were arranged. *This is in respect of the bereaved family members, for whom she thinks the chairs must be.*　行儀がよい to be well-behaved.　人目につかない場所で in obscure places, where unseen.　袖なしの、ワンピースから出ている肩と肩をくっつけて their shoulders touching, exposed from their sleeveless one-piece dresses.　相手の肩先に日焼けして、皮がむけているのを見つけたらしい seemed to discover that skin was peeling from the sunburn at the tip of the other's shoulder.　首だけを真横にねじって twisting her neck alone just beside her.　相手の肩の皮を、爪の先ではがしはじめた began to peel the skin from the other's shoulder with her fingernails.

待った、と私は冗談を言った。

二五 私たちは、スリッパにはきかえて、講堂に入った。小学生たちは既に整列して、式典のはじまりを待っている。子供たちを囲むまわりの壁には、被爆直後の写真が展示してあり、列の後には、椅子が並べてある。遺族席なのか、喪服を着た大人たちが坐っている。

二六 城山小学校の、被爆死した百三十一名の中には児童は数えられていない。夏休み中だったので、子供たちは自宅にいた。千四百名にのぼる子供たちは、自宅で被爆死している。親も子も、一家全滅の地域だから、喪服の大人たちが遺族だとすれば、奇蹟的に助かった人たちだ。

二七 私は、椅子が置いてある場所をさけて、入口に近い壁ぎわに立って式典を待った。中田も私と並んで立った。テレビカメラが入っているので、子供たちは行儀がよかった。おしゃべりをしている子供は見あたらない。私が小学生のころは、式がはじまる前には、鼻をすりあげる音が講堂一杯に響きわたったが、鼻をすりあげる者もいない。しかし、人目につかない場所で子供たちは、やはりいたずらをしていた。後から二、三番目に立っている二人の少女が、袖なしの、ワンピースから出ている肩と肩をくっつけて、どっちの肌が日に焼けているか、比べあっている。見比べているうちに、一人の女の子が、相手の肩先に日焼けして、皮がむけているのを見つけたらしい。首だけを真横にねじって、相手の肩の皮を、爪の先ではがしはじめた。皮をむかれている女の子も、自分の肩や腕の、皮が火傷もなく、皮がむけていないのを確かめると on assuring myself that I had no burns and no peeling. *Although there were fire burns from the wide-spread fires, the majority of burns were flash burns. The temperature at the hypocenter is estimated to have reached 3,000 to 4,000 degrees C at the hypocenter. A common symptom of flash burns was peeled skin hanging from arms as described in the next paragraph.* 一目散に at full speed, head over heels.

28. 両腕の皮が、湯びきのように白く縮まって垂れ下がっている中学生 a middle school boy, with skin hanging from both arms, white and crinkled like the skin of a vegetable dipped in boiling water. 痛か、いたか いたいよう、いたいよう it hurts, it hurts.

29. 三十二年を経過した光景には、くらべようのない開きがあった between that scene and this one thirty-two years later was a wide gap that refused any comparison. かげりのない子供たちの動作 unclouded (innocent) movements/behavior of the children. ことさらな、平和への感慨はわかなかった（湧かなかった）felt no sentiment in particular about the current peaceful condition (i.e., this "peace" we were all now supposedly enjoying). 平面な、対等な位置で [the day and today existed within me] side by side, in parity. あるがままを受け入れて生きることに慣らされたせいか perhaps because I had become used to living while accepting things as they came. 鈍になりつつあるようだった [my senses] seemed to be growing dull [toward both the original August 9th and this peaceful day].

30. もっと険があったはずだ it seemed to me [based on my recollection] that [her eyes] had been sharper.

31. 短く言葉を切った cut herself short. 暫く間をおいてから after a brief pause.

むけかけた箇所を探している。皮をむいたり、見比べている子供たちの動作を眺めているうちに、私は、八月九日の自分の姿を思い出した。あの日、焼け野原に立って、私は腕をなで、肩をなで、そっと頬を撫でてみた。火傷もなく、皮がむけていないのを確かめると、私は一目散に金毘羅山に向かって走った。

[二八]両腕の皮が、湯びきのように白く縮まって垂れさがっている中学生が、痛か、いたか、と独り言を言って、目の前を逃げて行った。

[二九]三十二年を経過した光景には、比べようのない開きがあったが、かげりのない子供たちの動作を見ても、ことさらな、平和への感慨はわかなかった。あの日と今日とが二つ並んで、平面な、対等な位置で私の内にあった。あるがままを受け入れて生きることに慣らされたせいか、八月九日にも、平和な今日にも、私の意識は鈍になりつつあるようだった。

[三〇]中田も、子供たちの様子に気がついていた。私たちは顔を見あわせて、微かに笑った。意味のない笑いだったが、中田は優しい目をしていた。中田の黒く大きな目は、少女のころにはもっと険があったはずだ。

[三一]式がはじまるまでに二、三分の間があった。私は辺りに聞こえないように、ご主人、大変だったのね、と悔みを言った。中田は、う?と短く言葉を切った。暫く間をおいてから、人が死ぬことには

**儀礼的な挨拶** a ritual phrase [meant for those of us who had seen many deaths].

32. **淋しいでしょうけど、頑張ってね** you must be lonesome, but don't lose heart—*said with the recent death of Nakada's husband in mind.* **ううん、と静かな声で、しかし頑固に否定した** Uh-uh, Nakada contradicted me, in a calm but resolute voice. *Nakada means she is not lonesome from the recent loss.* **人の命を数で比較するわけじゃないけど** I don't mean to compare people's lives numerically but. **六人も死んでいるから** (*lit.*) because as many as six [immediate family members] died [by the bombing]; because I lost six [family members to the bomb]. **標準語で言った** *Nakada normally speaks in Nagasaki dialect as does the narrator's mother, while the narrator, now a long time Kantō resident, uses the standard language.*

34. **知らんやったと** 知らなかったの？ *Nakada has gone back to Nagasaki dialect.* **話さんやったもんね** 話さなかったものね I didn't talk about it. **母と姉たちが死んだとよ** 母と姉たちが死んだのよ. **家が城山にあったろうが** 家が城山にあったでしょう？You know my house was in Shiroyama? **茫然として** stunned.

35. **開会の辞** opening remarks. **恰幅のいい** well-built. **壇上に立って** standing on the platform. **一礼をした** bowed [in respect for her audience].

36. **水晶の数珠を左手にかけて** with a crystal rosary on her left hand. **指先でさぐりながら** fingering (the beads one by one). **珠と珠がふれあって鳴る硬質な音を聞きながら** listening to the hard sound of the beads clicking against one another.

慣れているから、おたがいに、ね、と言った。少女のころよりも低い声で話す中田の言葉を、死者を大勢みてきた被爆者同士の、儀礼的な挨拶だと私は思った。

三二 淋しいでしょうけど、頑張ってね、と私は言った。中田は、ううん、と静かな声で、しかし頑固に否定した。そして、人の命を数で比較するわけじゃないけど、六人も死んでいるから、と標準語で言った。

三三 ええ、と私は聞き返した。六人も死んでいるから、と言う言葉の意味が、私には理解できなかったのである。

三四 知らんやったと、と中田が聞いた。知らない、と私は答えた。あのころ、あたしは話さんやったもんね、母と姉たちが死んだとよ、家が城山にあったろうが、と言った。私は茫然として中田の顔を見た。

三五 開会の辞を、男の教師が告げた。黒いレースの喪服を着た、恰幅のいい女性が壇上に立って一礼をした。校長先生よ、と中田が教えてくれた。ライトが校長の顔面を照らして、テレビカメラが廻りはじめた。

三六 中田は、水晶の数珠を左手にかけて、一つ一つの珠を指先でさぐりながら、校長の話を聞いている。珠と珠がふれあって鳴る硬質な音を聞きながら、私は、中田の言葉を思っていた。

37. 二学期の授業が十月から開始されると When the second trimester classes began in October. *Normally, the second trimester began on September 1.* 近郊の市や村の疎開先から from the nearby cities and villages to which they had been evacuated.

38. 本明川の流れにそった県道筋にあって on the prefectural road that ran along the Honmyō River. 通りすがりに on my way to [the station]. 声をかけた called aloud to her (*the custom in those days was for a child visiting a friend to call out from outside*); *声をかける also simply means to address or invite.* さわさわと (*onomat.*) with a rustle or sough. その水音が、人が、群がってついてくる足音に聞こえて the water sounding to me like the footsteps of people swarming after me. 怖さが達したころに about the time my fear peaked.

39. オカッパ bobbed hair, from カッパ (河童), river troll. 下駄音をたてて making clacking noises with her wooden clogs. ハンカチ handkerchief. カバン (鞄) school bag; brief case. 灯りの落ちつき具合 (*lit.*) how steadily calm the light was; the steady light. いつも決まって invariably; unfailingly.

40. 門司港 Moji Harbor, at the northern tip of Kyūshū.

三七 戦争が終わって、二学期の授業が十月から開始されると、長崎で家を焼かれた女学生たちは、近郊の市や村の疎開先から、汽車通学をはじめた。その中の一人に中田がいた。中田は、私と同じ諫早から通学をしていた。

三八 中田の家は、本明川の流れに沿った県道筋にあって、二階建ての、風呂屋のように大きな家だった。諫早駅の近くにあり、私は、通りすがりに毎朝声をかけた。当時、私たちは六時九分発の列車に乗っていた。冬などは、まだまっ暗である。外灯も、人通りもない道を一人で歩いていると、本明川の、さわさわと流れる水音が聞こえる。その水音が、人が、群がってついてくる足音に聞こえて、私は足を早める。怖さが達したころに、中田の家の灯りが見える。私は、大声で中田を呼んだ。台所の隣の部屋に灯りがついていて、声をかけると、女のひとが返事をする。

三九 灯りの中でオカッパの頭が揺れて、下駄音をたてて中田が出てくる。白い、木綿のハンカチに包んだ平べったい弁当箱をカバンと一緒に右手にさげて、駆け出してくる。女のひとの声の調子や、灯りの落ちつき具合からみると、声をかけるのを待っている様子なのに、いつも決まって、慌てて出てきた。

四〇 六時九分発の列車は、門司港から下ってくる夜行列車だったと思う。闇物資の買い出し客が多く、

**夜行列車** night train. **闇物資の買い出し客** buyers of black market goods. **乗り損なわないように、敏しょう** (敏捷) **に行動するのが先決で** our first priority being to move swiftly so we would not miss the train. **比較的空いている列車** a car that was less full. **前から三輛目** the third car from the front of the train. **浦上** the Urakami district in Nagasaki City. *It is the site of the Peace Park, the Urakami Catholic Church, and the former Nagasaki Medical College, now part of Nagasaki University. The Church and the Medical College are located to the east of the hypocenter on the same circle within a radius of 500 meters from the epicenter. In the Edo period, Christianity was secretly practiced in Urakami in defiance of the Tokugawa shogunate's bans. Recurrent persecution began in 1790. The fourth wave in 1867-73 was the most extensive, with the jailing and torture in 1867 of 64 Urakami Catholics and 110 in nearby Ōmura, leading to 60 deaths. In 1870, 2,810 adherents were exiled to other provinces, as were over 3,400 in 1867. Five years into the Meiji era in 1873, 1,930 are said to have returned to Urakami.*

41. **四年生に進級した、一学期の冬** the winter of the first trimester when we advanced to the tenth grade; *normally the first trimester begins in April, which makes the third trimester of the ninth grade more likely.*

42. **独身を通す** to remain single. **結婚するやろうね** 結婚するでしょうね. **漠然と** ぼんやりと; vaguely. **わたしはせんよ** わたしはしないわよ. **言下に否定した** denied at one word.

43. **嘘じゃなかよ** 嘘じゃないわよ. **ただ、結婚という未知な将来について、夢を交えながら希望を話しあいたい** we merely wanted to discuss our hopes intermingled with dreams about an unknown future called marriage. **浮き立った** buoyant; lively; cheerful. **それを中田から、はっきり否定されると** that being unequivocally rejected by Nakada.

44. **なぜさ** なぜなの？ **矢つぎ早に**（矢継ぎ早に）in rapid succession (originally from speedy placement of the next arrow on the bow after shooting).

列車はいつも満員である。座席に座れることはまずない。乗り損なわないように、敏捷に行動するのが先決で、私たちはホームを走って、比較的空いている列車をみつけて乗る。空いている列車は決っていて、前から三輌目の列車によく乗った。浦上の家を焼かれて、大草から通学をはじめた島も、三輌目の列車に乗ってきた。

四一 そのころ、私たちは三年生だったのだろうか。それとも四年生に進級した、一学期の冬だったのだろうか。寒い季節だった。

四二 ある朝、私たちは、将来結婚をするか、独身を通すかという話をはじめた。中田と私と、大草から乗ってきた島と、他に二、三人の同学年生がいたようだ。結婚するやろうね、と漠然と二、三人の者が認めて言った。中田と島の二人は黙っていた。私は、あなたも結婚するわよね、と中田に言った。中田は首をかしげて考えていたが、わたしはせんよ、と言った。うそ、と誰かが言下に否定した。

四三 嘘じゃなかよ、と中田が言った。

結婚をしてもしなくとも、私たちは、どっちでもよかったのである。ただ、結婚という未知な将来について、夢をまじえながら希望を話しあいたい、浮きたった話題が欲しかったのである。それを中田から、はっきり否定されると、私たちは面白くなかった。

四四 なぜさ、理由を言ってよ、一生涯?と矢つぎ早に質問をした。中田は質問には答えないで、あたし

45. 何とか本心を聞き出そうと、言葉をかえて誘いをかける私たちに as we used this and that word trying to somehow learn her true feelings. 声をそろえて大げさに驚いてみせた spoke in unison, gesturing great surprise. わけを話してよ tell us the reason.

46. 学生を代表する行事には必ず選びだされる she was always chosen for events at which to represent students; she was always chosen as a student representative for school events. 各課目が、むらなくできる [Nakada,] who managed every subject equally well. 何処かいじめたくなる要素がある there was something [about honor students like Nakada] that invited teasing. あまり出来のよくない私たち those of us who were not great achievers.

47. むきになって in dead earnest. かみしめていた唇 her lips that she had kept firmly closed. トラピスト Trappist convent. The Trappists (the Order of the Reformed Cistercians of the Strict Observance) reached Japan in 1896. *Two years after the founding of the first Trappist (Cistercian) monastery in Japan, Trappist Sisters founded their first convent in 1898 in Hakodate in Hokkaidō, the second in 1935 in Kakogawa in Hyōgo, followed by three more in 1953, 1954, and 1981.* 修道女 nun. 癇にさわる irritating. いい子でありすぎる the answer made her too good a child; i.e., it was the answer that a model child would give.

は結婚せんよ、と言い張った。ほんとうに?と私たちは、しつこく聞いた。

四五 本当さ、と中田も繰り返して答えた。何とか本心を聞き出そうと、言葉をかえて誘いをかける私たちに、中田の答えは変わらなかった。へえーと私たちは、声を揃えて大げさに驚いてみせた。周りに立っている乗客たちが私たちを見たが、気にとめなかった。

わけを話してよ、と言った。中田は唇をかんで、取り囲んでいる一人一人を見ていた。

四六 中田は、頭がいい女学生である。同学年生の中に人気があって、学生を代表する行事には必ず選び出される。各課目が、むらなくできる中田に勝てる者は、汽車通学生の中にはいない。ただ中田のように優等生タイプの少女には、何処か、いじめたくなる要素がある。それは中田自身が持っている性格よりも、むしろ、いじめる側にいる、あまり出来のよくない私たちの方にあるのかも知れなかった。

四七 中田は、珍しくむきになっていた。相手が真剣になればなるだけ、私たちは意地が悪くなった。中田は、我慢ができなくなったのだろう。かみしめていた唇を開いて、トラピストに言って修道女になるのよ、と強い口調で言った。女学生らしい、優等生らしい答えだった。純粋な少女期には、誰もが一応考えることだが、結婚する、と答えた私たちにとっては、癇にさわる答えである。いい子でありすぎる。

四八 中田は、結構いたずらをする。汽車通学をしている男子学生の名前もよく知っていて、品定めをす

48. **品定め** appraisal. **ばたばたと慌てる面をもっていながら** although there was a side of her that made her flap around in panic. **根気よく** patiently. **空きそうな席を見つけて** spotting a train seat that was likely to be vacated. **くりくり** (*mimesis*) くりくりとよく動く目 (eyes that move constantly), くりくりした目 (big, round eyes), くりくり坊主 (crewcut head).

49. **トラピストだって、あなたが** "Trappist! You, of all people?" **片っぱし**（片っ端）**から** one after another, systematically. **顔を伏せないで** without lowering her head. **泣かしてしまった後悔と、泣かしてしまった満足感が交差してあった** regret at (unintentionally) having made her cry, and satisfaction at (unintentionally) having made her cry were present, cut across each other; we had mingled feelings of regret and satisfaction.

50. **絶句する** to be at a loss for words. **終戦直後の、汽車の中の情景** that scene on the train right after WWII.

51. **声をたてる** to raise one's voice; cry aloud. **言葉の数々** numerous words. **記憶の底から盛りあがってきた** brimmed up from the depths of my memory. **かたくなに** obstinately. **いい切る** to insist with determination. **断ちきれない愛しさ** unseverable attachment.

52. **外地にいる父親だけを残して** except for her father, who had been in an overseas area then under Japanese domination. **肉親** immediate family. **察しようがない** I could not begin to imagine.

る。ばたばたと慌てる面を持っていながら、根気よく、空きそうな席をみつけて、一人だけ坐ってにこにこしている。それに、くりくりよく動く大きな目は、男子学生たちに人気があった。

四九　トラピストだって、あなたが、と私たちは言った。行くつもりでいる、と言う中田の言葉を、片っぱしから否定していった。中田はとうとう黙った。目の玉から涙がこぼれ落ちた。中田は顔を伏せないで、大きな目を見開いて泣いていた。涙をみて、私たちは、はじめて責めるのを止めた。泣かしてしまった後悔と、泣かしてしまった満足感が交差してあった。

五〇　六人も死んでいるから、という中田の言葉を耳にした瞬間に私が絶句したのは、終戦直後の、汽車の中の情景が浮かんだからである。

五一　涙をこぼしながら、最後まで声をたてなかった中田の表情と共に、泣くまで追い詰めたあの時の言葉の数数が、鮮やかに、記憶の底から盛りあがってきた。かたくなに結婚を拒否して、トラピストの修道女になるといい切った中田の心のうちには、被爆死した母や姉たちへの、供養の気持があったはずである。断ちきれない愛しさがあったはずである。

五二　一瞬の間に、外地にいる父親だけを残して、肉親の全員を亡くした中田の悲しみは、私には察しようがない。悲しみのやり場もない中田は、修道女になろうと思いつめていたのだろう。何よりも、自

**悲しみのやり場もない** not to know where to direct one's sorrow; not to know where to turn with one's sorrow. **思いつめる** to think intently; to take to heart. **責める** to press, reproach.

54. **訓示** address, lecture. **私は、知らなかったのよ、ほんとうに、と** 私は、「知らなかったのよ、ほんとうに」と. **他愛（たわい、たあい）ない意地悪** simple-minded nastiness. **弁解** excuse. **悔いは年月の経過を飛び越して、私を、いたたまれない気持ちに追い込んだ** (*lit.*) remorse, jumping over the passage of time of months and years, drove me to an unbearable feeling; slipping in time, unbearable remorse overwhelmed me.

55. **列車の中での会話を私たちと書いたが** though I ascribed the exchanges on the train to "us." **どれほど大勢の人間があの場にいあわせていたとしても** no matter how many people might have happened to be at that spot. **多弁な** loquacious. **口をはさむ** (*lit.*) to insert one's mouth; to interject. **だからなのだろう、という島への配慮** concern for Shima that perhaps this was the reason [for her silence].

56. **被爆者の不幸を、八月九日の共通の日に立って、同じ被爆者として苦しんで来たつもりでいた** I had assumed that, as a fellow survivor, I had been sharing the suffering of survivors on the common ground of August 9th.

分自身の悲しみから中田は救われたかったのだろう。

そんな中田を、私たちは責めた。

五三 灯りがついた部屋から返事をしていた女のひとを、私は、中田の母親だと思っていたが、そうではなかったのだ。

五四 校長の訓辞は、まだ続いていた。私は、知らなかったのよ、ほんとうに、と心の中でつぶやいた。女学生の、他愛のない意地悪だったのだ、とも弁解してみた。しかし弁解は弁解でしかなかった。悔は年月の経過を飛び越して、私を、いたたまれない気持に追い込んだ。

五五 私は、列車の中での会話を私たちと書いたが、どれほど大勢の人間があの場にいあわせていたとしても、私が言った言葉の重さには変りがない。結婚とか恋愛の話になると、誰よりも多弁になる島が、あのときは、全く口をはさまなかった。ね？と誘っても、島は話には加わらなかった。島も、母親と祖父母を浦上で亡くしているが、だからなのだろう、という島への配慮さえも私にはなかった。

五六 中田も島も、そして私も被爆者である。私は、被爆者の不幸を、八月九日の共通の日に立って、同じ被爆者として苦しんできたつもりでいた。しかし、私はあの日に、家族の、誰ひとりも亡くしてはいない。私は、彼女たちの何を知り、何を理解したつもりで今日まで生きてきたのだろうか。

**彼女たちの何を知り、何を理解したつもりで 今日まで生きてきたのだろうか** in the course of my life until today, what had I presumed to know and what had I presumed to understand about them?

57. **ちょっと坐らん** ちょっと坐らない？ **歯切れの悪い言葉遣いで** in an inarticulate expression; cf. 歯切れのよい crisp, articulate. **なんのこと** なんのこと？ What about?

58. **よかとよ** いいのよ it's okay. **知らんとはあなただけじゃなかし** 知らないのはあなただけじゃないし; you weren't the only one who didn't know. **話せば泣きとうなるけん** 話せば泣きたくなるから; [I didn't talk] because if I talked, I would have felt like crying. **頑張っとったさ** がんばっていたのよ. **なにを謝ると** なにを謝るの？ What's the apology for? **忘れとった** 忘れていた.

59. **浦上の天主堂** the Urakami Catholic Church, located to the north of Nagasaki Medical College. *The original Romanesque building, begun in 1895 and completed in 1914, was destroyed by the bomb. It was rebuilt in 1959 with steel-reinforced concrete. The remodelling with stained glass and red bricks was completed in 1980. Of its 12,000 members, 8,500 are estimated to have died in the bombing.*

60. **なりたかったとよ** なりたかったのよ. **天守堂** Cathedral; here the Urakami Catholic Church. **葡萄酒色** wine-color. **修道服** religious robe. **活発な足どりで** at a lively pace. **褐色に冬枯れした石垣の草** grass over the stone fence winter-seared to brownness; dry, brown winter grass over the stone fence. **柔らいだ**（和らいだ）softened; mild. **あこがれとったっさ** あこがれていたのよ. **行かんやったし** 行かなかったし. **通さんやったし** 通さなかったし. **独身を通す** to maintain celibacy.

五七 追悼式は終わった。中田が、ちょっと坐らん、と椅子を指して言った。私は、中田の後について椅子に坐った。知らなかったのよ、と私は歯切れの悪い言葉遣いで言った。なんのこと、と中田が聞いた。式典の前の、短い会話を忘れてしまって中田は聞き返したのだろうが、私には痛い質問だった。

五八 お母さまたちのこと、と私は言った。ああ、と中田は思い出して、よかとよ、知らんとはあなただけじゃなかし、話せば泣きとうなるけん、あのころは一生懸命頑張っとったさ、と言った。ごめんなさいね、と私は頭を下げた。中田が驚いた表情で、なにを謝ると、と聞いた。汽車通学のころのこと、と私は言った。中田は笑った。忘れとった、と言って中田は笑った。

五九 小学生のころから修道女になりたかったとよ、と中田は言った。城山町にあった中田の家から、浦上の天主堂は近く、子供のころ、よく天主堂に行って遊んでいたという。

六〇 冬になると修堂女たちは、葡萄酒色の修道服を着る。葡萄酒色の修道服を着た修道女たちが、活発な足どりで天主堂の坂道を降りてくる。褐色に冬枯れした石垣の草や、柔らいだ光に似合っていて美しい。あこがれとったっさ、と中田は言った。

トラピストにも行かんやったし、独身も通さんやったし、と中田は言って笑った。

六一 児童たちは退場してしまっていた。講堂には五、六人の大人たちが残って、壁に展示してある写真

61. **退場する** to leave the place [after an event]; exit the stage. **壁に展示してある** displayed on the walls.

62. **報道写真家** press cameraman. **進駐軍** the Occupation forces (*literally,* the stationed forces), a friendlier name chosen over 占領軍（せんりょうぐん）for the US occupation of Japan after WWII. **～の命令で** by the order of～. **発表が禁じられていた** publication was prohibited; censored. **二人が学徒動員で働いていた兵器工場** the arms factory where we [the narrator and Nakada] had been mobilized to work. **数点** a few items. *点 is used here as a counter for items on display, instead of the usual counter for photographs 枚（まい）or 葉（よう）.*

63. **画面を試すように見ている** she was scrutinizing the photo as if to test its surface. **肩越しに** over her shoulder. **ガレキ**（瓦礫）rubble.

64. **爆心地に向いた二面の壁と、屋根が吹き飛んでいて** the roof and the two walls, facing the epicenter, having been blown off. **閃光と、爆風の特徴が如実に現れた破壊現場の写真として** as a photo of the site of destruction, in which the characteristics of the flash and the blast was graphically revealed. **二、三回同じ写真を見ていた** I had seen this same photograph two or three times.

65. **うちが燃えてる** my house is on fire. *Nakada speaks in standard Japanese dialect here again.*

66. **声をころして** suppressing her voice. **肩をしぼめて、しっかり唇を押さえている指の間から嗚咽がもれた** she hunched her shoulders, and a sob escaped through the fingers that firmly pressed her lips (i.e., Shoulders hunched, she covered her mouth with her hands. Through them a sob escaped.). *The subject of the first phrase is different from the subject of the rest of the sentence.*

を眺めている。写真は、八月九日の被爆直後から、十月までの浦上を写した写真である。

六二 報道写真家が撮影したフィルムで、進駐軍の命令で発表が禁じられていた貴重な写真である。中田と私は椅子を立って、百枚ほど展示してある写真の一つ一つを、見て廻った。二人が学徒動員で働いていた兵器工場の写真が数点あった。

六三 説明文と写真を読み比べていくうちに、中田が、一枚の写真の前で立ち止った。顔を写真につけて、画面を試すように見ている。中田の肩越しに見ると、向き合った白い壁が二枚、ガレキの中に焼け残っている写真である。

六四 爆心地に向いた二面の壁と、屋根が吹き飛んでいて、両側の二面の壁だけが残った写真である。閃光と、爆風の特徴が如実に現われた破壊現場の写真として、私は二、三回同じ写真を見ていた。白壁の家は、どこかの大学の研究所に使われていたらしい。

六五 「どうしたの、と私は中田に聞いた。中田は黙って、白い壁と、説明文を指した。そして、「うちが燃えてる」と震える声で言った。見ると、白い壁の後方に、白い煙が昇っている。中田がいう、「家」はみあたらないが、確かに、何かが燃えている。それを中田は、あたしのうち、と指をさして言った。

六六 中田は両手で口を押えると、声をころして泣いた。肩をしぼめて、しっかりと唇を押さえている指の間から、嗚咽がもれた。それは悲鳴だった。

悲鳴 scream.

67. 印刷業 printing business. 火勢 fire's force. 焼け跡 the ruins of a fire. 遺体 the bodies.

69. 工場の鉄骨の下で under the factory's steel frame. 意識をなくして、倒れていた lay unconscious.

70. 私のように焼跡から逃げていないから not having fled the ruins on foot as I did. 被爆地の煙や焼跡の状況 the state of the smoke and ruins of the bombed area. はじめて目にする that she saw for the first time. 我が家 her own house.

71. 白い煙をあげて giving off white smoke. 中田に向かって言うべき言葉 words to say to Nakada.

六七　中田の家は、白壁の研究所の真裏にあったという。印刷業をしていて、紙や油があったので火勢はひどく、中田の叔父たちが焼け跡に遺体を探しに行ったが、近づけなかった。

六八　火は数日間燃え続け、まだ煙が立っている焼け跡から、中田の母と姉たちの骨を、叔父が拾って諫早に帰ってきた。

六九　兵器工場で被爆した中田は、工場の鉄骨の下で夕暮になるまで意識をなくして、倒れていた。助け出されて、汽車に乗せられて、そのまま、諫早よりも先の大村まで運ばれている。

七〇　中田は、私のように焼け跡から逃げていないから、被爆地の煙や焼け跡の状況は見ていない。中田もまだ、今日まで、家の焼け跡を訪ねたことはないという。

写真は、中田がはじめて目にする、我が家の焼け跡だった。煙だった。

七一　写真は中田の目前で、白い煙をあげて燃えていた。中田に向かって言うべき言葉は、私にはなかった。私は、泣いている中田の横に立っていた。

# 草木

中上健次

# Trees and Grass

*Nakagami Kenji*

NAKAGAMI KENJI (1946-92) was born in Shingū, a coastal city on southern Kii Peninsula in Wakayama Prefecture, into a complex family situation. The sixth child of Kinoshita Chisato, he had two half brothers and three half sisters from his mother's earlier marriage. Four younger half brothers and sisters came later. When his mother moved to live with Nakaue Shichirō in 1954, she took just Kenji with her. In 1959 when Kenji was thirteen, his half brother Kinoshita Ikuhei committed suicide. That same year Kenji's surname changed to Nakaue following his mother's formal marriage to Nakaue Shichirō. "Nakagami," used as a pen name, is an alternative reading of the same surname. Nakagami Kenji moved to Tōkyō soon after graduating from Shingū High School and began his writing career in earnest. In 1968, he met the literary critic Karatani Kōjin through *Mita bungaku* (Mita Literature, a journal published by Keiō University's Department of Letters) and, at Karatani's encouragement, began reading Faulkner.

Between 1970 and 1974, as an employee of a subsidiary company of Zennikkū (All Nippon Airways), Nakagami worked at Haneda Airport, cleaning airplanes and loading and unloading goods for a cargo airline. In 1973 he was injured while working at Haneda and was hospitalized. For two years after quitting the job at Haneda, he worked as a carrier at Tōkyō's Tsukiji fish market and as a forklift operator at a transportation company.

Nakagami was awarded the Akutagawa prize for his "Misaki" (The Cape) in 1976, a novella depicting the *roji* (alley), a Shingū community of *burakumin* (discriminated people). The alley continued to be the topos of his fiction as with *Karekinada* (1977, Withered Tree Beach) and *Chi no hate shijō no toki* (1983, End of the Earth, Supreme Time), and *Sennen no yuraku* (1982, The Joy of One Thousand Years). Blood ties in this community are a recurring theme in Nakagami's writing. Further north from Shingū is the Kumano district, a mountainous region that was revered as a dwelling place of the gods from earliest times and was a popular pilgrimage site. Along with the *roji* community, Kumano is central to many of Nakagami's works including *Keshō* (1978, Makeup), *Sennen no yuraku,* and *Kumanoshū* (1984, A collection of Kumano stories).

Nakagami also wrote stage plays and film scripts. In "Yōkyoku Hongū" (Hongū: a noh play), a traveller from an eastern province encounters, at one of Kumano's three major shrines, the spirit of the mid-Heian poetess Izumi Shikibu. *Himatsuri* (Fire Festival), the author's first movie script (released in 1985), became the basis of a novel by the same title (1985-87). An unfinished manuscript of a stage play version of *Nichirin no tsubasa* (1984, The Wings of the Sun) is included in the fifteen-volume *Complete Works of Nakagami Kenji*, published posthumously in 1996.

In 1990, Nakagami founded in Shingū a people's school called Kumano Daigaku to offer lectures and seminars for thinking about Kumano. Its principles were "no school buildings, no entrance exams, graduation at death."

Nakagami was an energetic traveller. Starting in late August 1979, he lived in Los Angeles with his wife and two daughters for four and a half months. He returned to the United States in 1982 for three months as a visiting researcher at Iowa University's International Writers Program, and again in 1986 for four months as a guest researcher at Columbia University. He also travelled to Korea, India, England, Ireland, the Philippines, Hong Kong, Indonesia, France, and Vietnam, among other places.

"Sōmoku," first published in 1975 in a journal called *Fūkei* (Landscape), was included in *Keshō* (Makeup, 1978) along with eleven other stories.

## WORKS IN ENGLISH TRANSLATION

"Jain (A Salacious Snake)." Juri Abe, tr. in *Southern California Anthology*, University of Southern California, April 1985.

*The Cape and Other Stories from the Japanese Ghetto*. Eve Zimmerman, tr. Stone Bridge, 1999.

*Snakelust*. Andrew Rankins, tr. Kodansha International, 1991.

Nakagami Kenji's work has also been translated into French, German, Dutch, and Korean.

1. *The central character is 彼 (he), and the wounded stranger he encounters in the mountain is 男 (the man). It is important to keep the two separate in reading this story.* **山中で男に会った** [he, i.e., the central character] met a man in the mountains. **大台ケ原** short for 大台ケ原山, the main peak of the mountain range that runs along the border of Mie and Nara prefectures, a sacred place in mountain religion from long ago and part of the present Yoshino-Kumano National Park on the Kii peninsula. Kumano, a mountainous area overlooking the Kumano sea, was revered as a dwelling place of the gods from early on. It is also known as a popular pilgrimage site with its three shrines (Hongū, Hatayama, and Nachi) and a center of Shugendō (mountain asceticism). **山の中腹** half way up the mountain (a short hour's walk to Ōdaigahara). **杉の根方に背をあててしゃがみ込み** sitting on his haunches with his back against a cedar trunk near its roots; *the subject is the man, not the central character.* **ふともも、ふくらはぎに折れた矢がくいこみ** broken arrows digging into the thigh and calf. **身を隠すにも、もう身動きがとれない様子だった** even if he wished to conceal himself, he seemed no longer able to move his body. **この熊野山中に棲む神か、と思った** he (the central characer) suspected that the man might be one of the gods that dwelled in the Kumano mountains. **ここには** here in Kumano. **片方の足の機能を損じた** who has lost the function of one leg. **イッポンダタラ** (一本韛) "One-legged bellows," the one-legged, bloodshot-eyed monster said to dwell on the border of Nara and Wakayama prefectures. ダタラ is ascribed to 韛(たたら), a large bellows used at forges and operated by four or so men stepping on it. *Since Kumano was associated with forges, this makes sense; but, as suggested by Ingrid Lee, a student from Taiwan, タタラ could be a corrupt form of 大太郎 (big boy), pronounced Datailang in Chinese and Daitarō in Japanese. Cf. 大太坊(だいだぼう、だいだらぼう), a monster son born of a human woman and a great serpent.* **片方の眼が、血膿で固まっていた** one eye was covered with hardened bloody pus. **彼は、幻だろうと思った** he (the central character) thought him (the stranger) a phantom. **縁あってなお遠く離れているもの** related yet nevertheless far distant. **彼もみた** he [the central character] too had seen [a close relative now far away]; *it was said that in these mountains one encountered dead kin; the central character too had seen [a vision of] one on this trip.* **じいんじいんと蝉の声がするだけになった自分の体のすぐかたわらを、近親のものは、通り過ぎた** the close relative had passed right by his [the central character's] body, which was filled with nothing but cicada cries, i.e., which by then was no more than a receptacle for the shrilling of cidadas.

# 草木

一

山中で男に会った。あと小一時間も歩けば、大台ヶ原に行きつく、山の中腹あたりだった。杉の根方に背をあててしゃがみ込み、肩で荒い息をしていた。左脚のふともも、ふくらはぎに、折れた矢がくい込み、血を流していた。男は、彼をみた。ずっと以前から、彼が歩いてくるのを知っていたらしかった。身を隠すにも、もう身動きがとれない様子だった。最初、その男を、この熊野山中に棲む神か、と思った。ここには一本足の、つまり片方の足の機能を損じたイッポンダタラと称せられる大きな神がいた。男は神ではなかった。ただ片方の眼が、血膿で固っていた。「どうしたのですか？」彼は男の前に立って訊いた。男は黙って首を振った。彼は、幻だろうと思った。山中で、よく人は、死んだ近親の者、縁あってなお遠く離れているものの姿をみた。彼もみた。じいんじいんと蝉の声がするだけになった自分の体のすぐかたわらを、近親の者は、通り過ぎた。それこそ魂の幻なのだろうと彼は思った。

2. **故あって傷つき申した** there being a reason, I was wounded; *archaic, samurai-like speech.* **彼をにらみつけた** the stranger glared at the central character. **下手なことをすると** if he [the central character] blundered; if anything went wrong. **喉元を噛みちぎるという構えだった** his posture indicated he was ready to tear him apart at the throat; *a posture typically associated with a wild beast like a wolf or tiger.* **水瓶** usually pronounced みずがめ; here the alternate pronunciation すいびょう or すいびん is preferred for the religious association. すいびょう was one of the seven basic items ascetics carried. **ひったくった** grabbed, *colloquial.* **キルク** cork. **破れて土埃でよごれた** torn and soiled with dust. **厚い生地の服を柔道着のように前をあわせて着ていた** wore a garment made of thick cloth with front flaps overlapping like a *jūdō* jacket. **人ともけものとも判別がつかない** it was difficult to tell whether he [the stranger] was a man or a beast. **思わず踏みしめた左脚から** from his left leg on which he inadvertently put his weight. **上背が彼をしのいだ** his [the stranger's] upper torso was superior to his [the central character's], the man was taller than him.

3. **敗れてしもうた** I was defeated though I didn't mean to be. *With* てしもうた *(a dialectal form of* てしまった*), the stranger's speech leaves samurai diction and begins to assume the color of the local dialect.* **男は杉の木に手をかけて、傷ついた自分の体をふがいないというように、言った** the man said, with his hand (s) on the cedar and sounding as if ashamed of his wounded body; ふがいない (不甲斐ない) literally means good-for-nothing, unworthy of expectations, faint-hearted. **左眼が潰れているのが、納得できないと首をふり、手で押さえた** he shook his head as if not yet comprehending that his left eye had been blinded, and pressed it with his hand. **ものの見事に** beautifully, unarguably. **やられた** I was done in; defeated. **敗れたら、しまいじゃ** once defeated, that's the end. じゃ *is a dialectal form of* だ. **伊勢** a place northeast of Ōdaigahara. **熊野の村** the Kumano villages, to the south of the mountain and near the southern end of the Kii peninsula, for example 新宮 (Shingū) at the border of Mie and Wakayama prefectures, the novelist's birthplace.

[二]「どうしたのですか？」彼はまた訊いた。

「故あって傷つき申した」男は唸るように言った。彼をにらみつけた。下手なことをすると、喉元を噛みちぎるという構えだった。彼は、男の前に屈み、腰につるした水瓶を差し出した。男は彼の顔をみつめながら、それをひったくった。キルクの蓋を歯で開けて飲んだ。唇からあふれこぼれた水は男のあごを濡らし、首筋を伝い、破れて土埃でよごれた衣服に流れおちた。短かい毛の生えた胸に、水がゆっくり流れ落ちるのが、破れ目からみえた。いや、破れ目ではなかった。厚い生地の服を柔道着のように前をあわせて着ていた。なにやら奇妙な生き物に思えた。人ともけものとも判別がつかない。男は空になるまで飲みつくし、そしてやっと水瓶を返した。男は深く息を吐いた。立ちあがろうとした。よろけた。思わず踏みしめた左脚から血が流れ出した。男は杉の木に背をかけて、立った。上背が彼をしのいだ。蝉の声が、遠くで聞こえた。杉木立の湿ったにおいがした。

[三]「敗れてしもうた」男は杉の木に手をかけて、傷ついた自分の体をふがいないというように、言った。水瓶を差し出すと言葉遣いは変っていた。左眼が潰れているのが、納得できないと首を振り、手で押えた。「ものの見事に、やられた。敗れたら、しまいじゃ。やられた、やられた」男は言った。わらった。

「どこへ行くのですか？」彼は訊いた。「伊勢の方へ行くのですか、熊野の村の方へおりるのですか？」

4. **わしに行くところがどこにあろかよ** おれに行くところがどこにあるものか wherever would I find a place to go? *あろかよ is a dialectal form.* **どこにもありやせん** どこにもありはしない there is none anywhere, *similarly dialectal.*

**どこであろと、のう、落ちてゆくわい** どこであろうと、なあ、落ちてゆくさ wherever it may be, well, I will plod along. *The verb 落ちる characterizes the man as 落人, a samurai fugitive fleeing for safety.* **けもののにおい** (獣の匂い) beast-like smell. **貨物に足をやられて** had his foot / leg banged up by some freight goods. *Recalls a leg injury the author suffered in 1973 while working at Haneda Airport. The anachronistic reference here to life in twentieth-century Japan ("freight goods" and "hospitalization"), is only one of several examples scattered throughout the story. The setting of the remote hills acquires an otherworldly sense not only from the mention of dead spirits and the juxtaposition of historically incompatible speech styles but the seemingly unremarkable encounter between the man and a half-dead samurai with broken arrows embedded in his thigh and calf.* **崖っぷち** the edge of a cliff. **ここに置いて先を行って下され** please leave me here and go on; *polite and slightly archaic.* **鴉がとびあがった** *crows are traditionally associated with death.* **それとも、いっそ、のう、ここから下へ放り込んでくれんか？** or, rather, now, why not do me the favor of hurling me down from here?—*here the stranger is speaking to his equal.* **そうやって自力で歩くことも動くこともできない自分がよほどふがいないのか** [the central character reasoned that] he [the stranger] must quite despair of himself, unable to walk or move on his own. **湯の出るところ** where there are hot springs (such as Shingū and Nachi Katsuura down south). **思案する時間を与えると、男は、山中で行き会った見知らぬ人間に救けられる心苦しさがわきあがるのだろうと** thinking that, if he [the central character] gave him [the stranger] time to think it over, the man [the stranger] would experience a surge of discomfort about being helped by an unknown person whom he had met in the mountains. **さあ、行きますか** well, let's go, shall we? **よろぼいながら** tottering. **崖のふち** the edge of the cliff; cf. 崖っぷち above.

「わしに行くところがどこにあろかよ。どこにもありやせん。いや、いや」と男はまた首を振った。「どこであろと、のう、落ちてゆくわい」男は一歩踏み出し、次の一歩が出ず、よろけてしまった。彼は、男を支えようと思って、手を差し出した。男は、激しく振り払った。男は尻餅をついた。杉の木に頭を打ちつけた。それでも彼は男にむかって手を出し、男の腰をかかえあげた。今度は、拒まなかった。腕を、彼の肩にあげてそれで男の体重を支えた。けもののにおいがした。それは人間本来のにおいなのだろう、彼が仕事場で貨物に足をやられてしばらく入院していた時、洗わない頭、股間からけもののにおいが立った。男を支えて、杉木立の中を歩いた。すぐ、崖っぷちに出た。白く明るい日が、崖の草木の緑を照らしていた。男の口から息がもれるたびにシュッシュッと音がした。男を岩においた。男は彼の顔をみつめ、それから、「ここに置いて先を行って下され」と言った。一羽、崖の下から、鴉がとびあがった。「それとも、いっそ、のう、ここから下へ放り込んでくれんか？」男は、唇を閉じた。そうやって自力で歩くこともできない自分が、よほどふがいないのか、と彼は思った。そこから山々のつらなりがみえた。果しがなかった。鴉が五羽、また下方から舞いあがってきた。湯の出る所まで二つほど山を越えなければならないはずだった。思案する時間を与えると、男は、山中で行き会った見知らぬ人間に救けられる心苦しさがわきあがるのだろうと、彼は、「さあ、行きますか」と声を掛けた。男を抱えた。二人で、よろぼいながら、崖のふちに残った道を

**蝉の声と、それにあわせてたてる男と彼の、息の音がした** the cries of cicadas and the accompanying sound of his and the man's breaths were heard. **左眼をこすっていた** (the man repeatedly) rubbed his left eye [that was wounded]. **あれこそ** that precisely; that bird, if not this man (could be a phantom).

5. **兄の法事** a Buddhist commemoration of his [the central character's] older brother. *This recalls the author's half brother who committed suicide when the author was thirteen.* **気づいたのだった** he recalled having noticed [that one of the finches was blind]. *Note the use of のだった here.* **巣立ちする** *also* 巣立つ, to leave the nest; (*fig.*) to graduate. **十姉妹** society finch, a kind of Japanese finch that is 10 centimeters long and smaller than a sparrow but with a thick beak. White with dark brown, black, or brown mottles; or all white. It was created from 檀特 (ダントク, see below), which was imported from China. Because it is skilled at brooding, it is often used as a hatching parent for other birds. *The author kept one hundred or so finches at home in late 1973.* **盲いていた** was blind, *a deliberate use of an obsolete expression echoing the reference to the man with a poor eye.* **栄養** nutrition. **それとも遺伝子の悪戯で、たまたま劣性がかけ合うことになったためか** or perhaps, due to pranks played by the genes, recessive genes happened to cross. **純白の羽毛だった** it had snow-white feathers. **親の種鳥** the breeding bird that was the father of this [blind] bird. **並の、つまり白黒のまだら** an ordinary, in other words white and black spotted, finch. **檀特** normally a kind of red flower resembling canna; here a kind of Chinese bird. From Sanskrit *dandaka*. 檀特山(だんとくせん) is the name of a mountain where the Buddha is said to have practiced asceticism either in his former life or when still a prince. **近親交配** incestuous crossing. **よく兄妹**(きょうだい, *alt.* あにいもと)**をつかまされる** one often is tricked into buying brother and sister birds. **元々、十姉妹など姿形を楽しむものでもないし、声を賞でるものでもない** to begin with, a bird like a finch is not enjoyed for its appearance or praised for its voice. **健康に……という雑草のたくましさが身上だ** to healthily chirp and hop, not mind a small amount of rough handling, lay eggs if there is a nest, raise its young, which become fully fledged in three or so months after leaving the nest—this kind of weed-like hardiness is its [sole] merit. **いっそ殺してしまおうか** perhaps it would be better if I made up my mind and killed it. *The expression いっそ (after all) is used when resolutely making a choice that is quite different after contemplating many alternatives, or when giving up a pleasant choice in favor of something much worse.* **指が、嘴に触ると、すぐ逃げた** when

降りた。またすぐに丈高い杉木立に入った。道は、崖をはずれた。耳に、蝉の声と、それにあわせてたてる男と彼の、息の音がした。男はしきりに右手で左眼をこすっていた。ふっと、彼は、東京に残してきた小鳥のことを想った。あれこそ、幻かもしれない。

五

兄の法事で熊野に来る直前に、気づいたのだった。この春に巣立ちした十姉妹の一羽が盲いていた。原因は何によるのかわからなかった。巣立ちの頃に栄養が欠けたためか、それとも遺伝子の悪戯で、たまたま劣性がかけ合うことになったためか。純白の羽毛だった。親の種鳥は、並の、つまり白黒のまだらだった。檀特からいま十姉妹に変異したというような健康なやつだった。近親交配のせいか、と思った。デパートの小鳥屋で買ったものだった。一つの店で雌雄を買うと、よく兄妹をつかまされる。いやな気がした。どうしようか、と思った。相手は人間ではなく、小鳥だ。盲いて生れた小鳥など、飼っていても、苦しくなるだけだ。元々、十姉妹など姿形を楽しむものでもないし、声を賞でるものでもない。健康にピッピッと鳴きとびはね、少々の乱暴も気にかけず、巣があれば卵を産み、雛を育て、巣立ちすれば三カ月ほどで一人前になる、という雑草のたくましさが身上だ。いっそ殺してしまおうか？彼は金網にとまったままの十姉妹を、つついた。指が、嘴に触ると、すぐ逃げた。合計十姉妹だけで何羽いるのだろうか、一メートル四方の十姉妹専用の雑居籠の留り木は、うずめつくさ

his fingers touched its beak, it [the blind finch] fled right away. 一メートル四方の十姉妹専用の雑居籠 the one-meter square mixed-residence cage for exclusive use by finches. うずめつくされていた was completely buried [by perching birds]. その中に割り込めず unable to edge in amongst [the perched finches]. すとんと下に落ち、うまい具合に餌台に立つ fell with a plop and, by good luck, found itself standing on a feeder. 瞳孔のあたりが白く濁っている it was opaque around the pupils.

6. 殺してやろうと思いつづけたのだった he recalled that he had kept thinking he would take its life [rather than let the blind finch suffer a life of mere repetition: perching on the wire netting, jumping, pecking at the bird food, drinking, and perching on the wire netting]. いっそこの世に生命を受けたことなど、なかったことにしろ Pretend that no such thing happened as that you were born in this world [that, after all, would be an easier choice]—*the central character is talking in his mind to the blind finch.* 籠の三方をおおった板に体当たりして下に落ちた colliding against the wooden boards that covered the three sides of the cage, (the birds) fell down. いつでもとびあがれる姿勢を取っていた (the blind finch) assumed a posture that enabled it to fly up at any moment. それではじめて、わけの分からないとてつもなく大きなものにつかまえられたと気づいたふうに as if for the first time made aware by this that it [the finch] was in the grip of something incomprehensible and preposterously large. いつかもそんなふうにして殺した he had once killed a bird in that way. もがく to writhe, flounder, struggle. セキセイインコ（背黄青鸚哥）budgerigar, a kind of small parakeet about 18 centimeters long, characterized by the yellow back with black bars, greenish-yellow belly, and yellow wings and tail. 羽毛をふくらませ、留まり木にもとまれず、よろぼうていた fluffing up its feathers, unable even to perch on a roost, [the bird] tottered. 枕許に置いた籠の底で at the bottom of the cage he had placed by his bedside. ただバタバタ翼を底板に打ちつけていた[the budgerigar] was merely banging its wings against the bottom board. いつの間にか眠り、不意に、めざめると、死んでいた he fell asleep before he realized it, and when he chanced to wake, the bird was dead.

れていた。盲目の十姉妹は、その中に割り込めず、すとんと下に落ち、うまい具合に餌台に立つ。瞳孔のあたりが白く濁っている。

[六]きれいな十姉妹だった。また金網にとまる。なにをみているのか、ぼんやりとしている。そのうち、体のむきを変え、とびおりる。餌台におりて、餌をついばむ。水を飲む。また金網にとまる。そのくり返しだった。殺してやろうと思いつづけたのだった。いっそこの世に生命を受けたことなど、なかったことにしろ。手を籠の中に差し入れる。十姉妹どもは騒いでまわった。金網に体をぶつけた。籠の三方をおおった板に体当りして下に落ちた。巣の後に隠れるものもあった。盲いた十姉妹は、籠の隅で、首をのばして立ち、いつでもとびあがれる姿勢を取っていた。彼の大きな手が、つかんだ。それではじめて、自分がわけの分からないとてつもなく大きなものにつかまえられたと気づいたふうに、翼をふる。もがく。逃げ出そうとする。日が当っていた。彼は、力を入れた。純白の羽毛の十姉妹はもがいた。そのまま力を入れれば、柔らかい骨の小鳥は潰れて死ぬはずだった。いつかも、そんなふうにして殺した。それはセキセイインコだった。買ってきても買ってきても、小鳥は死んだ。朝、仕事に出かける時、あんなにも元気だった小鳥が、夕、仕事から帰ると羽毛をふくらませ、留り木にもとまれず、よろぼうていた。籠を暖め、口を開けて、薬を飲ませた。夜、枕元に置いた籠の底で、立つこともできず、ただパタパタ翼を底板に打ちつけていた。いつの間にか眠り、不意にめざめると、

そんなことをみるに耐えず、嘔吐をくり返し、苦しみ悶える小鳥を、手で握って窒息死させた unable to bear seeing such a thing, he smothered to death in his hand the bird [the last of his budgerigars] as it repeatedly vomited and writhed in pain.　安楽死 euthanasia; easy death.　ただみたくなかった (not that he administered euthanasia; he simply did not want to see [the bird suffer.]　知恵の備わった人間だけで充分だった he thought it sufficed that (such a thing as suffering) was [an experience] limited to humans equipped with wisdom.　あまりに小さすぎた [the finch in his hand] was too tiny, i.e., too tiny to have to be killed. 盲いていることに、無頓着すぎた it was too nonchalant about its being blind.

7. 彼は大きな体の男だった he was large-bodied. *This brings out the contrast between his largeness and the little finch. It also makes the stranger in the Kumano mountains quite tall (see no.2).*　無骨な（武骨な）boorish.　華奢な delicate. 巣引きをする for a kept bird to make a nest.　ほのぼのともしよう it may even be heartwarming.　それが、死穢や奇形、変異にみまわれることがないならばだ but that's if the bird is not visited by death's pollution, deformation, or mutation, *which is not the case with this blind finch.*　翼をぴったり背にくっつけている held its wings firmly against its back [ready to fly at any moment].　なにものかを念じ、呼んででもいるように as if praying to, and calling, someone. 留まり木にひしめき（犇めき）、金網にとまった [the healthy ones] jostling on the perch or lighting on the wire net.　その十姉妹を中心にして centering around that [blind] finch.　餌をついばむ（啄む）to peck at the feed.　磁力をその純白の羽毛から発しているように見える seemed as if to radiate magnetic power from its snow white feathers.

8. 錦華鳥 "brocade flower bird," a kind of bird, multicolored and smaller than a sparrow, originally from Australia.　種鳥 mating bird.　どうせ、と思い、ほうっておいた he left them [the eggs] alone, thinking he wouldn't be able to help them anyway.　臆病な easily scared.

死んでいた。そんなことをみるに耐えず、嘔吐をくり返し、苦しみもだえる小鳥を、手で握って窒息死させた。安楽死ではなかった。ただみたくなかった。苦しむことなど知恵の備わった人間だけで充分だった。彼の手の中の十姉妹は、あまりに小さすぎた。盲いていることに、無頓着すぎた。彼は、籠の中に、もう一度十姉妹をもどした。

七 彼は大きな体の男だった。他人には、小鳥の飼育に熱中するようなタイプにみえなかった。人は、彼がその大きな武骨な手で小さな華奢な小鳥の世話をしている図は、童話の〝わがままな巨人〟のようだと言った。確かに巣引きをしている小鳥と、それを見守っている彼の姿は、おかしくもたのしくもある。ほのぼのともしよう。それが、死穢や奇形、変異にみまわれることがないならばだ。籠の中で、餌箱のへりに立ち、餌を食べることもなく、いつでもどこかへとびあがれるように首をのばし、翼をぴったり背にくっつけている。なにものかを念じ、呼んででもいるように、白く濁った瞳孔をこちらにむけ、盲いて生れた十姉妹はとまっている。留り木にひしめき、金網にとまった健康なやつが、その十姉妹を中心にして餌をついばみ、水を飲み、とびまわっているようにみえる。磁力をその純白の羽毛から発しているようにみえる。

八 錦華鳥を種鳥の籠と雑居籠の二つに分けていた時のことだった。雌一羽、雄四羽の雑居籠の中の巣に、卵が産まれているのを知っていたが、どうせ、と思い、ほうっておいた。臆病な鳥だった。物音人影をさえぎるために金網に紙を張りつけても、せっかく長いことかかって抱いて自分でかえした雛を、物音を聞いてあわてふためき、巣から蹴り落としたり、巣草の中に隠す even if he pasted paper over the wire netting to screen them [the birds] from a human figure, flustered by the sound [of an approaching human], the birds would kick from the nest, or conceal in the nesting grass, the young [from the eggs] they had so diligently hatched after brooding for so long. 毛虫同然の姿だった they [the young] were no different from hairy caterpillars. うっすらと血をにじませて（滲ませて） tinged lightly with blood. 割ってみもしないで without even trying to crack [the eggs]. もののついでと thinking it just an additional thing in passing; as long as I have gone so far; on the spur of the moment. ひく、ひく、と 動いた flitter-fluttered. 息を呑んだ held his breath. 手のひらの中で、外気にさらされても even when exposed to the air in my palm. 小さいものの心臓の鼓動そのままに precisely reflecting the small thing's heart beat. 毛頭 (*with the negative*) not at all. He had absolutely no intention of killing [the bird]. これは過ちだ。過ちだ。許してくれ this was an error, just an error, forgive me—*spoken to the life inside the egg*. 仏か、神か、それとももっと別のものかもしらんが、赤むけのむきだしの生命にむかって、この罰当たりのおれを許してくれ "I don't know if you are the Buddha or a god or yet some other being," [he said] to the red, naked life, "but forgive me, the accursed." 赤むけの flayed and raw flesh showing. むきだしの bare; uncovered. じいんじいんと脈打ちうずいている throbbing and tingling with pain. 「発心集」*Hosshinshū* (A Collection of Religious Awakenings. Compiled around 1213-1215), ascribed to Kamo no Chōmei (鴨長明), *the author of Hōjōki (方丈記, An Account of My Hut, ca. 1212). Nakagami Kenji quotes from Section 30, in which a messenger brings some food to a poverty-stricken Mount Hiei priest. The priest is profoundly moved to hear that his mother in the capital had sold her hair to procure the food for him. The narrator comments that even birds and beasts demonstrate parental love, and concludes the section with an example of a dog. Someone who was fond of falconry shot the dog to feed his bird. The dog turned out to be pregnant, and because the skin of her belly was shot through, a puppy or two spilled out. The mother dog started running for her life but returned, tried to run again this time with the puppies held in her mouth. She fell and died right there. The incident led to the religious awakening of this man, who dropped falconry and retired to his native village.* 鷹飼い falconer. 経験を同じゅうする share the same experience. 母犬の裂かれた腹からみえたのは……そのものだ what was visible from the mother dog's slashed belly was the life itself of some red flesh that had not yet even

ひとつしても、籠の中を大騒ぎしてとびまわった。人影をさえぎるために金網に紙を貼りつけても、せっかく長いことかかって抱いて自分でかえした雛を、物音を聞いてあわてふためき、巣から蹴りおとしたり、巣草の中に隠す。雛は死ぬ。そんなふうにした、何羽雛が死んだかわからない。まさに毛虫同然の姿だった。落ちて頭にうっすらと血をにじませて死んでいるのもいた。その雑居籠を掃除したついでに、卵をとりのぞいた。割ってみもしないでそのまま二個、ゴミ箱にほうり込んだ。もののついでと、一つを割った。中で、赤い肉が、ひくひくと動いていた。思わず息を呑んだ。手のひらの中で、外気にさらされてもまだ小さいものの心臓の鼓動そのままに、ひく、ひく、と動いていた。殺すつもりなど毛頭なかった。これは過ちだ。過ちだ。許してくれ。彼は言った。仏か、神か、それとももっと別のものかもしらんが、赤むけのむきだしの生命にむかって、この罰当りのおれを許してくれ。日の光を、この時ほど痛く強く体に感じたことはなかった。自分の生命がむきだしになり、日と空気にさらされて、じいんじいんと脈打ちうずいている。そんな風に過って卵を割ってしまったのは、四度ほどあった。そのまま孵化しても、盲いて生れるかもしれないが、「発心集」にあらわれた鷹飼いの話など、ほとんど彼と、経験を同じゅうする。母犬の裂かれた腹からみえたのは、まだ皮膚もつくることのない赤い肉の生命そのものだ。血が忌わしいのではない。肉そのものが忌わしいのではない。母の腹の暗がりの中にいて生命を形づくった、その小さいものの、無垢な、ひくひくと動く、生

formed a skin. 忌まわしい odious; abominable; offensive; accursed. Not that the blood was odious, nor that the flesh itself was odious. 母の腹の暗がりの中にいて……忌わしい what was odious was the untainted, flittering life itself of that little thing that stayed in the gloom of the mother's belly and formed into life.

9. 蝉の声が幾重にも重なっていた (*lit.*) cicadas' cries overlapped in multiple layers—*the story goes back to the mountain scene*. 息を吐き吸っているかのように as if breathing in and out. 汗が眼に膜を張っていた perspiration filmed the eyes. 梢 treetops. まだ暗がりにいるところを、いきなり日にさらされてひくひくと動くのはこのおれだ (*lit.*) that which flitters, abruptly exposed to the sun while still in the dark, is me myself. *The central character, who was reminded of the blind finch by the wounded man, now identifies himself with both the man and the bird.* 露出した岩をよけ avoiding bare rocks. わき水（湧き水）spring water. なだらかな坂 gentle slope. ここへ置いていって下され please leave me here—*still polite*.

10. どうして救けようとする？ why try to save me?—*direct style; a mixture of direct and somewhat archaic or dialectal polite forms characterizes the man's speech from here on.* 彼は黙って…… *the subject is the central character.* まだるっこしく finding the process too slow; feeling impatient. ひととき、我を忘れていた for a while, he forgot himself; he was carried away [drinking and cooling off]. 首を振った [the man] shook his head [declining water offered]. 腹を脈打たせていた the man's belly was pulsating. 左眼にふ（触）れぬように気をつけ taking care so as not to touch the man's left eye. 垢とも土埃ともつかぬものがこびりついた顔 his face caked with something that could be defined neither as grime nor dirt. たっぷり水を含ませて soaking [the towel] with plenty of water. すまん sorry; thanks.

命そのものが、忌わしい。

九　蝉の声が幾重にも重なっていた。いや、男と彼の息の音が、まるで、耳のそばで幾千幾万の人間が、いま、息を吐き吸っているかのようにきこえた。男の体は重かった。汗が眼に膜を張っていた。彼が反対に男に抱えられ、山中を歩いているように思えた。左眼を潰され、左脚を損じたのは自分だ。杉木立が続いた。日は真上にあるのに、梢で遮られていた。盲いて生れたのはこのおれだ。まだ暗がりにいるところを、いきなり破られ、日にさらされてひくひくと動くのはこのおれだ。この肉だ。露出した岩をよけ、ふらふらと歩いた。そこから丈低い草の生えたなだらかな坂になっていた。わき水の横に男をおろした。「ここへ置いていって下され」男は言った。「どうして救けようとする？」

一〇　彼は黙って、わき水を飲み、頭をぬらし胸をぬらした。まだるっこしく、腹這いになり、頭をつっ込んだ。ひととき、我を忘れていた。なんどもなんども頭に水をかぶった。男があごをあげ、荒い息を吐いていることに気づき、水瓶に水をくみ、差し出した。男は首を振った。呻いた。腹を脈打たせていた。彼は水を男の顔にかけた。それから、彼は腰に引っかけていたタオルを取って水にひたし、男の顔をぬぐった。血膿で固まった左眼にふれぬように気をつけ、垢とも土埃ともつかぬものがこびりついた顔をふいた。たっぷり水を含ませて、男の脇の下、腹をふいてやった。「すまん」と男は言っ折れた矢のくい込んだところをぬぐった he wiped the man's leg where the broken arrows dug in.　矢尻が肉にのめり込み、手でつかむこともできないくらいで二つとも折れていた the arrowheads thrusting themselves deep into the flesh, both arrows were broken off so close that it was impossible to hold them in the hand.　みせねば 見せなければ.　手のほどこし様がなくなる it will be too late.　なにをやってきたのだろう what had (this man) done before coming here?　誰がやったのだろう who had hurt him?—*these questions occur in the mind of the central character.*

11. さあ行くぞ we're on our way. *The central character's speech is less formal here.*　とび（鳶）kite.　拒んだ the man resisted.　左目が潰れ、左足は動かない。男は、呻いた。このまま動かずに、こうした草の中にいたい "My left eye is blind, and my left leg does not move," the man groaned. "I want to stay here as I am in the grass like this without moving"—*the words in quotation marks are the man's internal speech, or the central character's interpretation of the man's internal speech. No quotation marks are used in the original. The distinction between the two characters' thoughts becomes blurred, as the perspective of 彼 begins to overlap with that of 男.*　このままこうしていると if you stay here like this. *This and the following three sentences form an internal speech by the main character, addressed to the wounded man.*　化膿する to become infected.　発熱する to develop a fever.　痛くうずく to tingle / throb with pain.　むらがる to swarm.　ほじくる to dig up; pick.　～を啄ばむ to peck at ～.　空に舞い上がる [having done that, the crows will] fly up to the sky.　崖をまわり込む形で、おりた they descended while circling around the cliff; まわり込む *is an unusual expression.*　わき出た水でこけ（苔）の生えた岩 rocks on which moss grows due to the spring water.　男は、ほとんど重さを感じなかった the man hardly felt any weight / the man's weight was hardly perceptible [to 彼]—*perhaps deliberately ambiguous.*　二人の息の音が、彼には、以前にも増して数えきれないくらいになったのを知った he [the main character] realized that even more than before the breathing sounds of the two men were, to him, nearly countless.　ぞろぞろ群れをなして in droves.

た。男は誰かに似ていると思った。思い出せなかった。タオルを水で洗いなおし、折れた矢のくい込んだところをぬぐった。矢尻が肉にのめり込み、手でつかむこともできないくらいで二つとも折れていた。すぐにも外科医にみせねば、手のほどこし様がなくなる。いったい、この男は、なにをやってきたのだろう。誰がやったのだろう。わからなかった。空で、とびが舞っていた。音はなかった。まだ一つの山を半分も越えていなかった。

「さあ行くぞ」彼が言った。男を抱き起こした。拒んだ。蟬が鳴き交いはじめた。左眼が潰れ、左脚は動かない。男は、呻いた。このまま動かずに、こうした草の中にいたい。このままこうしていると、傷が化膿し、体が発熱し、吹いてくる風にさえ痛くうずき、生命は果て、腐る。鴉が体にむらがる。眼球をほじくり、腹を破り、肉を啄む。空に舞いあがる。男は、彼に支えられて立ちあがった。彼はまた、男をかかえて歩きはじめた。自分が歩いているのではなかった。形をもたない赤むけのひくひく動く肉が、もうひとつ赤むけの傷ついた肉をかかえて歩いていた。なにも考えなかった。なにも感じなかった。崖をまわり込む形で、おりた。わき出た水でこけの生えた岩をまたぎ、かすかに一本残っている道を歩いた。男は、ほとんど重さを感じなかった。二人の息の音が、彼には、以前にも増して数えきれないくらいになったのを知った。ぞろぞろ群をなして、赤むけの傷ついた肉をかかえて、肉が歩いていた。後にもいた。声がきこえた、男は呻いた。坂を降り、すぐまた木立の中にはいった。

男の声は割れて笛のようにひびいた the man's voice, cracked, sounded like a pipe. どこのかたか存じませんが I don't know where you are from but—*a common way of addressing a stranger, polite and slightly old-fashioned; the rest of his speech here is crudely imperative.* 眼一つ脚一つにされた reduced to being one-eyed and one-legged. そこの杉にこの頭を打ちつけてくれえ bang my head against the cedar there as as a favor. 岩をめがけてつきおとしてくれ toss me down aiming at a rock. 男をなだめようと so as to coax / pacify the man. 色の変わった左脚をのばし stretching his left leg that had become discolored. 右脚をたてて、バネにし lifting his right knee to use it as a spring. いざりより、むきを変えようとして体の平衡を失い、男は横倒しになった sidling up closer and trying to change bodily direction, the man lost his balance and fell sideways; *いざる (to move on one's knees) and いざり (the physically handicapped) are both obsolete.* 一人で死ぬこともできん I can't even take my own life.

12. 声を殺して suppressing the sound. 現 reality. 幻 vision; hallucination; phantom. 敗れたというのなら、彼もそうだった if the [wounded] man had been defeated, so had he [the main character]. 大きな体の男だった *the same statement was made about the main character earlier in the bird episode, but here this can refer to either the central character or the wounded man [who is the taller of the two], bridging the previous sentences in the same paragraph where the subject is the main character and the next two sentences where the topic is the wounded man.* ひびきこもる resounded within [the mountains], *a beautiful, unusual combination of ひびく (to resound, echo), which is an outward motion and こもる (to be confined <in>, to stay inside), which is an inward motion; both terms are often associated with 山 as in やまびこ (echo) and やまごもり (secluding oneself in the mountains).* 山全体が、敗れ、やられて、片眼、片脚になり、それでも自死すら出来ぬ男の、声でいっぱいになる the entire mountain became filled with the voice of the man who had been defeated, wounded, lost an eye and a leg, and yet was unable even to take his own life. 彼の体まで、楽器のように鳴っている even his [the main character's] body was ringing like a musical instrument.

日が空でかげったらしく、光はなかった。いきなり、男が泣き出した。「ここで、殺してくれ、ねがいだ」と叫んだ。「頼む、頼む、殺してくれ」男の声は割れて笛のようにひびいた。「どこの方か存じませんが、眼一つ脚一つにされたおれを殺してくれ。首をしめてくれ。そこの杉にこの頭を打ちつけてくれえ。岩をめがけてつきおとしてくれ」男は叫んだ。男をなだめようと杉の根方に背をもたせかけ、坐らせた。色の変った左脚をのばし、右脚をたてて、バネにし、男は後頭部を杉にむかって打ちつけた。いざりより、むきを変えようとして体の平衡を失い、男は横倒しになった。「一人で死ぬこともできん」男は言った。男は口をあけた。下の歯が全部欠けているらしかった。男は涙を流した。

一二「いったい誰にやられたのですか？」彼は訊いた。男は、黙ったままだった。

彼は立っていた。横倒しになって、手で顔をおさえて、声を殺して泣く男をみていた。村の者にやられたのだろう、それとも何百年もの前の戦で敗れたのだろうか？その敗れた者の魂か？彼はわからなかった。それが現なのか幻なのかわからなかった。敗れたというのなら、彼もそうだった。やられたというのなら、彼もそうだった。大きな体の男だった。男のもらす泣き声が、山中で、何倍もの音量でひびきこもる。山全体が、敗れ、やられて、片眼、片脚になり、それでも自死すらできぬ男の、声でいっぱいになる。彼の体まで、楽器のように鳴っている。

一三 泣き続ける男のわきに坐り、杉に体をもたせかけ、しばらくその音をきいていた。梢と梢が重なり

13. ひょろひょろと柔らかに育った草 slender, tender grass. 男の声、息の音に呼応して in response to the man's voice and breathing. 共鳴 sympathetic vibrations. 生命の本の本 the ultimate source of life. それはものも言わず、聴えず、見えず、感じもせず、考えもさせぬこの闇、その光だ it [the ultimate source of life] is this darkness, its light, that neither speaks, hears, sees, feels, nor allows thought. 男の泣き声に共振れする自分の体、自分の骨に恍惚となりながら ecstatic over his [the main character's] own body and bones that resonate with the man's wail. ある日ある朝、庭の土をほじくっていると出てきた発芽寸前のソラマメのように like the kidney bean plant that came out when, one day, one morning, he [the main character] was digging the dirt in his garden, *a parenthetic phrase*. 木立がかかえた湿気た空気 the moist air that the trees held. あたうる限り（あたうかぎり／あとうかぎり） as much as possible. シダの胞子さながら just like a spore of fern. 泣きながら、眠り、目覚めては泣いた (the main character) slept while crying, and each time he woke, he cried. おまえはあの兄か、それともあの男かと問うた asked himself if he was that older brother of yours [who had taken his own life] or that man [the wounded man]. そうだ……われわれだ yes, it is we who caused the man/ourselves to lose the left eye, to be wounded in the left leg, and to be unable even to commit suicide. 生命のとった形か？ the form that life took? そして彼は、みた and he saw [in his reverie]. 法事 Buddhist memorial service. なむあみだぶつ(南無阿弥陀仏) incantation of the name of the Amida Buddha. 和尚の声が一区切りするたびに each time the priest's voice [reading the sutras aloud] paused. 口々に唱和した invoked [Amida's name] in unison.

合い、震え合い、鳴るのだった。日が射さないために、ひょろひょろと柔らかに育った草が、男の声、息の音に呼応して鳴るのだった。蝉の声が、共鳴するのだった。山全体が、いま男に合わせて、泣いているのだった。彼はしばらく、そうしていたかった。そうしていると、卵を割って見つけた赤むけの肉のような彼の体が、あらたにいまいちど破け、生命の本の本が、あらわれてくる。生命の本の本、それは物も言わず、聴えず、見えず、感じもせず、考えもさせぬこの闇、その光だ。闇はいっぱいある。彼は、男の泣き声に共振れする自分の体、自分の骨に恍惚となりながら、ある日ある朝、庭の土をほじくっていると出てきた発芽寸前のソラマメのように、手足を屈め、体をまるめていた。杉のにおいと泣き声と木立がかかえた湿気た空気の中で、自分があたうる限り小さく変化するのを知る。そして、シダの胞子さながら、吹きぬけてくる風にふうっと浮かぶ。彼は男と共に泣きながら、眠り、めざめては泣いた。おまえはあの兄か、それともあの男かと問うた。眠った。そうだ、左眼を潰し、左脚をそこない、もう自死すらできぬ具合にしたのはわれわれだ。このおれだ。だがしかし、このおれとは、なんなのだ。生命の取った形か？そして彼は、みた。山の下、熊野の母の家で、法事が行われていたのだった。なむあみだぶつ、なむあみだぶつ、なむあみだぶつ、と集まってくれた近隣の人は、和尚の声が一区切りするたびに口々に唱和した。人々は背をまるめ、身をちいさくしていた。母は和尚のすぐ後に坐っていた。ほうぼうから戻った姉たち三人はすぐ横にいた。義父と義父の子と、

**ほうぼうから**（方々から）from various places. **義父** stepfather. **仏壇にともしたろうそくの火** the flames of the candles lit on the household mini-altar. **いっこうに有難さの分からぬ和尚の読経** the priest's sutra reading whose merit he [the main character] didn't appreciate at all. **焼香** incense-burning ritual. Attendants at a Buddhist memorial take turns to offer incense for the repose of the dead by adding with respect a small amount of incense flakes three times from the container to the burner. **それは幻だ** that [the memorial scene in which the main character sees himself among the attendants] is an illusion. *The main character tells himself that he is having a reverie, and that his real self is in the mountains, now asleep, now awake, crying in resonance with the wounded man.* **心筋梗塞の発作** a stroke of cardiac infarction. **阿弥陀如来** Amida as one who comes from the absolute truth, another name for Amida, from Amitabha Tathagata (*Sanskrit*). **母をこそ、せめて自然に、草が立ち枯れるように死なせてやりたい** [I don't care about the wounded man, big brother, and myself;] I wish to let mother, if not others, at least die naturally like a blade of grass withering in place—the main character's internal speech. **宗旨の違う法華経** the Lotus Sutra, of a different religious sect [than the family's]. *The Lotus Sutra is the basis of the Nichiren sect, whereas the family seems to uphold the Pure Land sect with its emphasis on Amida.* **よし、おれが、行く** okay, I'll be the one to go [die]—*the brother's line*. **くびれて死んだ** hanged himself. **自分が死ねば、すべてが治まる** if I die, everything will be fine—*the brother's line*. **ことあるごとに** on every single occasion. **魂呼ばいの巫女にでもなったように** as if they had become mediums who invoke the spirits of the dead. **それ以降** from then on. **兄と彼がシャム双生児にでもなったように彼をみるたびに、兄を呼んだ** 兄と彼がシャム双生児にでもなったように、彼をみるたびに兄を呼んだ as if he and his older brother had become Siamese twins, each time his mother and sisters saw him they invoked the spirit of his brother.

彼がいた。仏壇にとぼしたろうそくの火が黄色く赤くみえた。いま、法事が行われている。母の家で、彼は、いっこうに有難さのわからぬ和尚の読経に耳を傾け、なむあみだぶつ、なむあみだぶつと小声で唱えている。読経がとぎれ、焼香をはじめる。そうだ、それは幻だ。この山中で男の泣き声に共振れをおこし、泣いて、眠り、めざめてはまた泣いているのが、彼だ。母は、肥りむくみ心筋硬塞の発作で黒ずんだ顔をあげ、阿弥陀如来の御名を唱え、それから、焼香する。彼は母をみている。男のことも、兄のことも、いい。自分自身のことも、いい。母をこそ、せめて自然に、草が立ち枯れるように死なせてやりたい。母は焼香を終えると、姉たちに、かすかにけむりの立つ焼香の盆をまわす。次々焼香する。彼もする。和尚の読経は続いている。突然、彼は思い出したのだった。いまの彼の齢より若い兄が、この仏壇に宗旨の違う法華経を一時間ほど唱え、よし、おれが、行く、と言い、次の日早朝くびれて死んでいたのを。自分が死ねば、すべてが治まる。それからことあるごとに、姉たち、母たちは、魂呼ばいの巫女にでもなったように兄の名を口にした。母や姉たちは、まるで盲いた十姉妹のようなものだった。それ以降、兄と彼がシャム双生児にでもなったように彼をみるたびに、兄を呼んだ。

一四　男はいた。もう泣いてはいなかった。日が、杉木立の上で、暮れかかっているらしく、寒かった。湿気が、鼻先にここちよかった。男は、杉の幹に背をもたせかけ、坐っていた。男の息の音は、静か

14. **男はいた** *The main character wakes from his visionary recollections and perceives that the wounded man was still there.* **いまさっきまで** until just a while ago.

15. **救けは受けとうない** 救けは受けたくない I don't want to be helped / saved. **このまゝ置き去りにして下され** please just leave me alone here. *The ending して下され is polite and archaic.* **それともいっそ殺してくれ** or even better, kill me. *The language echoes an earlier passage. There, the narrator recalls thinking of killing a blind bird; here the wounded man with a maimed eye asks the narrator to kill him. See no. 5.* **おれが誰であろうかよ** おれが誰であろうはずもない、おれなど誰でもない how can I be anybody? *The interrogative ending かよ is colloquial.* **乞食** beggar. **かったい** an older form of かたい(乞丐), which is also archaic, meaning beggar, leper.

16. **馬鹿げたことを言って** don't talk nonsense. **おぼろげに** （朧げに） vaguely; hazily. **ほれ** look; listen—*similar to ほら.* **声が掛かる** voices call, fall [on the central character's ears]; cf. 声をかける (to invite). **ざわざわと音をたてる** (*onomat.*) makes a rustling noise.

だった。いまさっきまで、自分の肉、骨が楽器のように、男の泣き声に共振れをおこしていたことが、不思議だった。梢から、湿気が水玉となって落ちていた。ぽと、ぽと音がした。「あと、一時間もすれば、川に出ます。川沿いを歩けば、村にいきつきます」

[一五]「救けは受けとうない、このまま置き去りにして下され、それともいっそ殺してくれ」

「あなたは誰なのですか？」彼は訊いた。男は黙った。弱くわらう声がきこえた。

「おれが誰であろうかよ。この山に這いまわる乞食、かったいの仲間よ」男は言った。「名前などない」

「あなたを救けたい」

[一六]「馬鹿げたことを言って」男は、言った。声が闇の中で、響いた。日はすっかり落ちてしまっていた。さっきまでおぼろげにみえていた杉の木の形も、いまはなかった。滴がしきりに落ちていた。「それよりもいっそこのおれを殺してくれ。この先何年も何年も、こんな体で生きていくのは心苦しい。殺してくれ」男は言った。「ほれ」と言葉をつぎ、黙った。「聞えるか、村の方から、また、おれを呼ぶ」男は言った。彼の耳にも声は、聞えた。方々から、老若男女のものらしいいくつもいくつもの声が掛る。その声の波に合わせて、山が、ざわざわと音をたてる。梢がうごき、彼の足を置いたあたりの草が、むずむずと身をもちあげる。地面がぼこぼこっと音をたてて動く。ふっと息苦しくなる。

むずむずと (*mimesis)* with an itchy or creepy motion. ぼこぼこっと (*onomat.*) with a bubbling or hollow sound. 彼は聞いた he [the main character] listened. まぎれもなく(紛れもなく) unmistakably. 里の村へおりて行って、言ってくれ go down to the home village and tell them—*here the wounded man assumes the persona of the main character's dead brother.* 今さら母が苦しんでなんになる what good does it do for mother to suffer pain at this late point. 嫁いでいった left home to marry, *slightly archaic.* 母や妹たちを苦しめるために、くびれたんではない I didn't hang myself to make them suffer.

17. おれのことはいい don't worry about me. 男のお前に [so I am asking you for a favor,] you as a man; *(1) the wounded man makes a man-to-man request, (2) and in doing so unwittingly suggests the main character's identification with him.*

18. 兄やんねえ、覚えてとるかあ You're my big brother, aren't you, do you remember me? *The sister's and mother's speeches are dialectal.* かわいもんよ lovely thing; dear son. 若い身空で at your young age. *身空(みそら) is used in reference to a sympathizable personal circumstance, while 身(み) by itself is neutral.*

19. おれは、おまえを救ける I'm going to save your life. *The main character now speaks as if to his close peer or inferior.* 要らん no need; I don't want you to. 喉を圧し潰し痛みに耐えきれぬ呻きをあげた he [the wounded man] let out a strangled groan, unable to bear the pain. むっくりと with an abrupt motion (applied to something round or plump).

「ほれ、あの声。あの声があるために、夜は寝れない」彼は聞いた。それはまぎれもなく、母の声だった。姉たちの声だった。「里の村へおりて行って、言ってくれ。もう苦しむな、もう忘れろ、と。いまさら母が苦しんでなんになる。嫁いでいった妹たちが苦しんで、なんになる。母や妹たちを苦しめるために、くびれたんではない。母や妹たちが幸せになるように、くびれた。おれのことは忘れて、幸せに生きろ」

一七「その代り、あんたが、左眼を潰され、左脚を損じて苦しんでいる」

「おれのことはいい」男は黙る。「だから、おれは頼んでいる。男のお前に。殺してくれ」

一八　その時、声がした。それは、姉の声だった。「兄やんねえ、覚えとるかぁ」と聞えた。それから母の声もした。母は、呻いていた。「おまえが、首つって、すぐ家に運び込まれ、母さんが顔みたら、赤い鼻血がたらたら出てきたねえ。かわいもんよ。なんで若い身空で首つって死んだ？みんな、母さんが悪かった。母さんが一番悪かった」母は泣く。

一九「おれは、おまえを救ける」彼は言った。立ちあがった。男の腕をつかもうとした。「要らん」と男は振り払った。ざわざわと音がした。梢が鳴った。喉を圧し潰し痛みに耐えきれぬ呻きをあげた。おう、おう、とけもののように男は唸った。彼の耳のそばで誰かがむっくりと起きあがる気配がし、ひた、ひたと音をたてて、木立の下を歩いていく。「ああ、かわいもんよ、なんで死んだ」母の声に合

**ひた、ひた** (*onomat.*) the sound of lapping water, quiet yet hurried footsteps. **人の世に生まれなんだら**（うまれなかったら）**、よかった** it would have been better had I not been been born to this world–*the wounded man's line.* **風にさらされ** exposed to the wind. **あれは、兄の生まれ変わりか？** was that bird a rebirth of older brother? *The red flesh of the unborn bird, associated with that of the fetus in a female dog as well as with the stranger and the central character, is now equated with the older brother who had commited suicide.* **死んだ子の齢をかぞえる** to count the years of a deceased child—*a set phrase.* **死んだものを想うことは要らん** no need to miss (long for, crave, have thoughts about) the dead. **器量よしのその顔が、台無しになる** your attractive face will be spoiled. **彼の目に涙がたまる** tears collect in his [the main character's] eyes. **あれから、死をまっとうに**（真っ当に）**死ぬことも出来ず、こうやって傷つき山中にうずくまっていたのか？** has he [the big brother=the wounded man], unable even to die his death properly, been crouched in the mountains like this ever since?

20. **干乾びて**（干涸びて、乾涸びて）dried up. **まさに、穀断ちを行ったのと一緒だった** it was precisely the same as having fasted / it precisely coincided with his [the main character's] fasting [while walking through the mountains]; *grammatically ambiguous. The second reading lends a religious meaning to the main character's walk in the Kumano mountains.* **穀断ち** refraining from [eating] grains, i.e, living on nuts and grass roots for the purpose of religious training or fulfillment of a prayer. **しばらくそうやって** keeping the same posture, i.e., with the dead bird still on his palm. **日の光が、へんに優しいのを知ったのだった** he perceived that the sun was oddly gentle.

わせるように、男は、おう、おう、と呻く。「もう忘れてくれ。人の世に生れなんだら、よかった。忘れてくれ」彼は、痛みを耐えきれぬ男の呻き声を耳にし、その小さいものの、ひくひくとうごく赤い肉を思い出した。なにもわからず、なにひとつ知らず、生命は風にさらされ光にさらされ、うごく。あれは、兄の生れ変りか？「里の村で、母に伝えてくれ。なにひとつ苦しむな、忘れろと。病に苦しめられ、そのうえに、死んだ子の齢をかぞえて苦しんで、なんになる。母が泣く。妹の、泣く声がする。死んだ者を想うことは要らん。器量よしのその顔が、台無しになる。生きよ。身も心も魂も夫に預け、兄のことは忘れろ。生きてくれ」彼の眼に涙がたまる。凍りついた闇の中で、彼はいま、十何年前に死んだ兄と向い合って杉の根方に坐り込み、しゃべっている。あれから、死をまっとうに死ぬことも出来ず、こうやって傷つき山中にうずくまっていたのか？

二〇 法事を終え、東京にもどってきた彼は、その盲いて生れた小鳥が、雑居籠の四つほどある巣の一つに足をひっかけ、干乾びて死んでいるのをみつけたのだった。まさに、殻断ちを行ったのと一緒だった。足にまきついた糸をほどき、手のひらに乗せてみた。彼はしばらくそうやって固く干乾びたそいつをみていた。日の光が、へんに優しいのを知ったのだった。

# 電車の中で読書する人々

多和田葉子

## 場所

この町の人たちは、家では本を読まない。図書館でも本を読まない。電車だけが読書の唯一の場所なのである。電車の中では、人は名前がないので、時間がたっぷりある。

## 仮面

電車の中で本を読む人たちには変な癖がたくさんある。たとえば、本を鼻に近づけすぎる。本は顔を隠すためにあるのかと思ってしまうほどだ。本は、それを読む人の顔に、第二の名前とひとつのタイトルを与える仮面のようなものかもしれない。

## 嗅覚

本を読みながら眠ってしまった人は、文字から立ち上ってくるにおいをかいでいるようにもみえる。

## 手話

本を支えている指の形は、ひとりひとり違っている。指は何かを言おうとしている。それは本の内容とも関係がないし、読んでいる人の性格とも関係がない。指たちは、人間には理解できない会話を勝手に進めている。その手話は、電車の中で交わされる隠語のようなものだ。

釣り人

右手の人さし指を耳の穴に突っ込んで、本を読んでいる人もいる。本の中から聞こえてくる声以外の声を聞かないですむように。その人さし指は時たま、耳の奥から記憶を釣り上げる釣竿となる。

重層構造

日の光が本の表面にさし、樹木のかげが右から左へ滑っていく。文字は上から下へと流れる。樹木と文字がページの上で正面衝突を起こすことはない。だから、本の表面にはいくつもの層があるのだということが分かる。

謎

子供が、本のページをいろいろな角度から眺めている。あたまをちょっと傾げるたびに、くちびるに微笑みが浮かぶ。子供は先へ進もうとはせず、同じページにとどまったままだ。頭を少し動かすだけで、違う物語が現れるらしい。

覗き

本を読む人の右隣りに座っている女は、本の方を見ないようにしている。まるでそうしなければ好奇心を抑えることができないとでも言うように、女は右の方ばかり見ている。隣に座っている人の本を盗み読みするのは、電車に乗っている人間のすることの中でもっとも恥ずかしいことだとされている。誰でも、覗き魔だとは思われたくない。同じ本を図書館で見たとしたら、興味を引かれなかったかもしれない。電車に乗っていると、誰でも、普通なら絶対読まないような本にまで興味を感じる。

広がり

電車がどんなに混んでいても、本さえ読んでいれば狭くてやりきれないということはない。本のページが、読書する人のまわりに無限の空間を広げる。

連帯感

子供達が、羊のように人体を押し付けあいながら立っている。どの子供も自分の本を読んでいる。子供達は口をきかず、ますます強く体を押し付けあいながら読んでいる。

未練

ページをめくったばかりの子供の人さし指が、もう読んでしまったページに張り付いたまま、離れようとしない。視線は先へとすすむのに、指はいつまでもそこにとどまっている。その文章を忘れるのがいやなのだ。話がよいほうに展開していくのだと分かっていても、悲しい文章から離れる気になれないのだ。

統合

制服を着た五人の子供たちは、みんな同じ高さに本を支えている。誰も本の高さなど気にしていない。子供たちではなく、本たちがお互いを見つめあい、連帯しているのだ。その統一は、人間が無理やり足並みを揃えようとするときのように、ぎこちなかったり、冷酷であったりはしない。

夢

本を読む人の隣で居眠りすると、その本の主人公に夢の中で出会うことがある。居眠りしていたその人が、ある日どこかで偶然同じ本を読むと、初めて読む本なのに、主人公に以前どこかであったことがあるような気がして、おやっと思う。

硬質

本を読みながら肌が石のようになっていく女がいる。すると、目も鼻も口も閉じて、顔の中へゆっくりと消えていく。真珠の首飾りと指輪だけが輝きを増していく。

飛翔

電車の中で読まれる本は、つかまるところがない。机の上に置かれているのではなく、空中に浮いている。自分のあるべき高さを見つけることができずに、上がったり下がったりしていることもある。

祈り

電車の中で読まれる本が小さいときは両手が背表紙のところで組み合わされ、読んでいる人は、そんなつもりはないのに、お祈りしているような格好をすることになる。本が鼻の高さにあるときは祈りは天の神々に捧げられ、お腹の高さにあるときは地の神々に捧げられる。

どこか

視線がちょっと活字を離れることもある。視線は空中をさまよい、何も見ることができないまま、本のところへどもってくる。他の乗客たちなどというものは、本を読んでいる人の目には、透明人間のようにしか見えない。視線がさまよってきた空間は、電車の中にあるのではなく、どこか全く別のところにある。

眼球

目の動きをまわりの人たちから保護するために、本を読んでいる間は、まつ毛がいつもより長くなる。目の玉は見えない。ただ、目の脇の小皺が現れたり消えたりするので、視覚器官が働いていることが分かる。

女と男

若い女達は、兵隊のように直立不動の姿勢で読書している。背広を着た会社員達はたいてい、上機嫌の猫のように背中を丸めている。男女が隣り合わせて坐って本を読んでいる。女は背筋を伸ばして座り、男は猫背である。ふたりは、くちびるひとつ動かさない。電車が止まると、女は急に口を大きく開けて、あきれたように言う。あたしたち、おりないと。そういわれて、男は隣で本を読んでいるのが自分の妻であることを思い出す。

高校生

二人の高校生が一緒に一冊の本を読んでいる。片方が、ページをめくってもいいかと視線で尋ねる度に、もう片方は首を縦に振ったり横に振ったりする。彼らは、ベッドに並んで横たわっているようにもみえる。本がベッドを思い出させるのは、本もベッドも夢をみる場所だからかもしれない。

綱渡り

痩せた男が片手で電車の扉の取っ手に捕まって読書している。綱渡りの男の話でも読んでいるのだろう。ページをめくっている間も、体が右へ左へと揺れる。額には、汗の玉が浮かんでいる。

眼鏡

年配の婦人が読書用眼鏡をかけて本を読んでいる。眼鏡のグラスはふたつの層に分かれている。下の層を通して見えるのは生き物のような活字であり、上の層を通して見えるのは銅像のような乗客たちである。

変換

視線は暴力かもしれない。本はその視線を受け止めて、文字に変換する。

子ども

乗客のからだが小さければ小さいほど、その手の中にある本は大きい。大人の読んでいる本は、子どもの絵本に比べると、とても小さい。ごく幼い子どもが、巨大な絵本を開く。それは、テングかテンシが翼を広げているところのように見える。電車は混んでいたが、それでもまわりの大人たちはできる限り、開かれる絵本のために場所を空けてやった。本を読むという行為には、こんなにも広い場所が必要なのだ。

# 辞書の村

多和田葉子

一

暦を驚き騒がす教会の鐘が鳴る朝の五時に。がらんがらんと風が吹く。アラスカ鮭やカラスや林檎が、頭でっかちの樹木の枝から、ばらんばらんと振り落とされる。やわらかい土に、丼型の穴が開く。

二

その村には出来事というほどの出来事もない。その村は辞書の中から生まれた。だから、その村では突飛な物も驚くには値しない。場違いであっても恥じる必要がない。辞書の中に出てくる単語たちが、でてくる順番に、現実のものになって、そうして村ができ上がった。村ができてしまうと、それが何語の辞書であったのかは忘れられてしまった。辞書は自分の腹の中から単語が全部抜けてしまうと、蝉の抜け殻のようになって、翌日から降り始めて止むことのなかった秋雨に濡れて飴のように溶けてしまった。表紙のない辞書などというものは窓の無い空と同じで、一度溶けてしまえば歴史に残ることもなく忘れられてしまう。

三 この村には心を騒がせる事件は起こらなかった。だから、たとえば教会の鐘のような大きな音だけが興奮を引き起こし、うまくいけば、退屈しきった大使たちを陶酔状態まで持って行ってくれるかもしれなかった。大使たちは職業柄、退屈しやすい。大使は町に住むのが当然で、村に住んでいるはずがない。しかし辞書の村には確かに大使がいる。そんなところがまた辞書の村らしいところだ。

四 村の人間たちの性格は穏やかである。家の庭にテーブルを置いて、家族が集まって牛乳を飲んでいる。大型のビールジョッキで、喉を鳴らして飲んでいる。ビールのような臭い飲み物は好まれない。ビールという単語がたまたま糞尿という単語の隣にあったため臭くなってしまったのかもしれない。牛乳の表面には泡がたっていて、それは中性洗剤の垂れ流しで汚染された川を思い出させる。テーブルクロスは真っ白だ。お父さんの目の玉も白いし、お兄さんの耳も真っ白。この家族は色素を否定して暮らしている。少なくとも以前はそれが徹底していた。俺の飲んだ母乳は、草の緑色をしていて苦かった、と叔父が得意そうに話し始める。あの頃は、何もかも白かったわけではないのさ。いろいろな自然の不調があって、災害もあって、色が出たりしたものさ。辞書の村では、自然と言う言葉が誰かの口から漏れると、なんだか居心地の悪い雰囲気が広がり、必ず誰かが咳をする。

五 それは、五十年前の雨の降らない夏のことだった。地面に生えていた草がみんな枯れてしまったので、草の精たちは行き場がなくなって、いろいろなところに勝手に宿り始めた。その夏に生まれた赤子たちは、みんな緑の乳を飲んで、性格に共通した特徴が現われた。まず、感情がアルカリ性に片寄りがちになった。これは気をつけないと、巨大な嫉妬や借金を生み出したりする。緑が緑にもつれて、身をふりほどこうとすればするほど、からまってくる。もちろん、そんなことは誰も口に出しては言わないが。他人の攻撃に立ち向かうビタミンは充分あるが、葉緑素が自己満足を呼び起こし過ぎて、深刻な話し合いの最中に急にサンドイッチを鞄から取り出して、平気な顔で齧り始めたりする。人の言うことにはあまり耳を傾けず、そのくせ日和見主義者なのだ。その年は緑の年と呼ばれた。その年に製造された洗濯機で洗うと、白い下着はみんな緑色に変ってしまうのだった。その年に収穫された葡萄で作ったワインは、赤ワインも白ワインも例外なく緑色だった。その年に書かれた本は、作者がどんなに抵抗してみても、表題に〈緑〉という言葉が入ってしまうのだった。緑の航海日誌、緑町の色女、きつね緑とピンクりす、忘れられた緑の太陽、赤坂から緑坂まで、緑が丘殺人事件、中小企業の緑営化。

六 緑の年の話をする時の叔父は機嫌がいい。話の種のつきた時は、みんな叔父に緑の年の話をさせようとする。話の種も植物の種と同じで、どんな季節にも、ぱちぱちはじき出されてくるものではない。誰も何も言わない季節というものがある。そんな季節には、コーヒーカップも音をたてない。音のない日曜日は恐ろしい。あまりの静けさに膝をがくがくさせながら、叔父が父親と喧嘩を始めるのも、この静けさの中にみんなが沈んでいってしまうのを見るのが怖いからなのだ。アーチ型の背中を持つろばと、遠洋漁業船の中で木こりとして働くこととどちらが寂しいかなどと言う問題について、長々と議論し合うのもそんな時だ。

七 この日、去勢された目覚まし時計が現われた。息子が新しく買ったオートバイにそういう名前を付けて乗り回すことに決めたのだ。静けさを恐れるあまり叔父と父が頭の中から捻り出す議論には息が詰まりそうになる。でも静けさは耐え難い。だから風もないのにカーテンが震えるように踊っているのだろう。静けさから耳を救ってくれるのは機械の音だけだ。これは月曜から土曜まで息子が仕事場で使っているドリルと同じ音を出した。息子は道路工事をしていた。オートバイは、ドリルと同じ音を出しても道に穴を開けることはない。ドリルも本当は穴を開けているわけではない。なぜなら、辞書の国の地表は紙で、その下には何もないからだ。

八 息子は、村を突き抜けて走る舗装道路をオートバイで飛ばしたが、村から遠く離れることはなかった。道端でスカートの縁を風に遊ばせている女性がいても息子はハンドルを握る手をゆるめなかった。恋愛をしたいと思ったが、女性と口をきくのは嫌いだった。恋愛をして、好かれるにはどうしたらいいのかと、息子は祖母に尋ねた。すると返ってきた答えは、マッコウクジラの脳味噌から取った香料が必要だということ。クジラを殺してしまうくらいならば、恋愛などしなくてもいいくらいクジラが可愛い。だから、クジラが使い捨てた脳を捜しに行かなければならない。でも、クジラはいらなくなった脳味噌をどこに捨てるのだろう。そもそもクジラという単語はどこに住んでいるのだろう。昔ならばクジラは川に住んでいたので、船の中から手を伸ばしてその背中に触ることもできた。今は両岸を埋め立てられて川が狭くなって、クジラは山の中にしか住んでいないので、山に登らなければならない。

九 息子はオートバイに乗って、山の裾野まで走った。それから、山に入るにはまず登山電車に乗るのです、と警官に教えられた。警官は怪しい人間にはみんな親切に道案内をしてやって、そうしながら、その人物をくわしく観察するのだった。ポケットから歯ブラシがのぞいていれば、朝帰りということになるが、それは犯罪ではない。虫歯がないだけましだ。警官の探しているのは、もっと恐ろしい記号を背負った男たちである。そういう男たちは警官と顔を合わせずに電車に乗り込んでしまう。

密輸業者の下っぱが、登山電車の中で口論していた。首の無い人形を輸入することは禁じられているが、それは船の中で首を縫いつけて、港で税関を通り抜けたら、その首を切り落とせば、それでもう立派に密輸になるのである。なると思ったのだ。人生経験の浅い下っぱは。ところが、縫いつけてしまえば、人形の首というのはそう簡単に切り落とせるものではない。ハサミは折れるし、指は腫れ上がるし、目は燃え上がる。それを見て人形はけらけら笑う。ボスは怒って、靴を脱いで窓ガラスに投げつける。結局経費は予算を上回って、人形は売れず、従って儲けが全くないどころか大損をしたところへ、山へ登って、〈類似したひとつの物〉を取ってこいという命令が下がった。何と類似したものなのだ、と尋ねても、そんなことは自分で考えろ、とボスはどなるだけ。登山電車の切符は高い。これだけのお金があれば、ポップコーンの入ったスープでもチョコレートのフライでも食べられたのに、と思いながら電車に乗ったチンピラはむしゃくしゃするのでガムを噛んでいるうちに、同じ電車に乗っていた鞄売りの青年と喧嘩になってしまった。人の喧嘩を見物するほど楽しいことはないので、みんなもっと公共の場で喧嘩すればいいのにと思う。そう思う人間はたくさんいるらしい。だからこそ大道喧嘩屋という職業があるのだろう。鼻の頭にひまわりの種から取った脂を塗って、膝を三回軽く打てば、喧嘩の心構えはできる。ちょっとでも拍手が起こると、もう嬉しくて緑色の唾が唇の間から染み出してしまう。しかし登山電車の中にはそんなにたくさん人がいるわけではない。喧嘩するふたりの他には、オートバイから降りて鯨を捜しに行く青年がいるだけだ。

二

やがて喧嘩は終わった。星座をやわらげながら、夜の縁側にすわっている不良青年たちのように、三人並んですわって煙草を吸っている。オートバイの青年とチンピラと鞄屋。職業は違っていても、喧嘩の後の煙草の味は同じ。彼らの性格は穏やかで、どこから風が吹いてきても、首をちょっと傾けるだけで、死体のにおいは避けることができる。注射器の針の太さを思い浮かべながら、密輪の袋に手を差し入れる。ひとつきりしかない魂を考えると、さすがに目をつむって注射を打つ気にはなれない。砂糖を肉に打ち込めば、家が焼ける。草の汁を血管に注ぎ込めば、カエルがいっせいに鳴き始める。平和の庭で腕立て伏せをしながら、オートバイの青年は歯を食いしばった。これではどうにもならない。どこかに出口があるはずだ。ひとつの道を走り始めても、道そのものが機械や動物でできているから目的地に着くことなどできない。恋をするつもりだったっけ。鞄に恋をしてうずくまると、舗装道路にも温もりがある。月の光が畔道を高速道路にする。ちょっとあんた、あんたでしょ、そう呼びかけられて顔を上げると、半端者の女が月の光に照らされて立っている。半端者というのは、身体の右半分がぼんやりとごまかしたようにかすんでいて、無いも同様なのだ。青年は、ある言葉を言いかけて途中でやめた。自分もやっぱりこうなのだろう、と青年は思った。この自分も言いかけてやめた言葉のようなものなのだ。そのせいか、クジラの捨てた脳味噌を捜して歩いていても、まるで人生に目的がないように思えてならない。

# Zという町

多和田葉子

一 毎朝、眠りのドアを開けて目を覚ます。それが同じひとつのドアなのか、毎日違うドアなのか分からない。目の前にあるドアは普通一枚だから、それを押す。すると、その向こう側にある、目覚めという名前の世界に出る。

二 しかし、その朝わたしは間違ったドアを開けてしまった。いつもならドアの取っ手の隣には「押す」と書いてある。それが、その日は「とびかかれ」と書いてあったので、あわててとびかかったのがいけなかった。しかも、そのドアは、手が触れると、中心から上下ふたつにカクンと折れて、あっと言う間に、それが又左右にバキッと折れて、その四分の一になったドアがまた八分の一にボリボリ、そして、最後には本の大きさになって、わたしの手の中にあった。わたしはその聖書のように分厚くて小さい本を持っていくべきかどうか迷った。結局、証拠に持って行くことにした。これがなければ誰も、わたしが眠りの中から間違えたドアを開けたために、Zという町に出てしまったのだと話しても信じてくれないだろうから。

三 それが夢であると言うのならば、目を覚ませば自分の町にもどることができる。しかし、わたしは目覚めることによって、Zという名前のこの町に来てしまったのだから、どうすればZを出ることができるのか分からない。しかも、わたしは強制的にここに連れて来られてしまったわけではなく、わたしの憧れを象徴しているのがZだからZに来てしまったのだということは、自分でも充分承知している。

四 憧れていると言っても、別にZにある何かが特に見たいというわけではないし、Zにいないと何かが欠けているという感じもしない。憧れというのは、焦がれの一種で、それはただ、肌が沸騰して、ぶつぶつ言って、それで焦げてしまうという感じなのだ。その感じには、名前もないし、実体もない。取り敢えず、その憧れというものにわたしがZという町の名前を付けたのは、それは町というものも、実体がありそうでないものだから、というだけの話だった。焼けて焦げる時に、その痛みを、Zという名前の町に行きたい、という希望に翻訳すれば、どうにか痛みも耐えられる。町に着いた時には、それなりの満足感もある。着くのは大抵、中央駅だ。だから、普通は、駅というのは落ち着かない場所で、麻薬常習犯が捨てた注射の針が足の裏側に刺さらないかと心配しながら、なるべく足早に通り過ぎたい場所なのだけれども、Z駅の場合は、さあ欲望を満たせる場所へ到着しましたよ、と言うように、じっくり迎えいれてくれる。駅には、床屋もシャワー室も郵便局も喫茶店も本屋もある。だから、髪の毛を切ることもできる。爪や髪の毛が伸びた時にそれを切りたいという欲望ほど強いものはない。墓に埋められてからも爪や髪は伸びるが、それを気にして死人が墓から出て来たりしないように、棺桶にハサミを入れておくのはそのためである。爪や髪を切りたいという気持ちがなくなったら、自分の肌への執着も薄れる。駅には、郵便局もある。手紙を出したいという欲望も強いもので、わたしは手紙がふたつ折りにされて、それから四つ折りにされて、封筒という袋の中に入っていくところを思い浮かべただけで、もうじっとしていられなくなり、手紙を書くことがよくあった。そして、その封筒には、Zという町の名前だけが書かれている。人の名前も番号もない。手紙は、憧れであるZそのものに直接送られていく。

五 しかし、自分の憧れの中に彷徨い込んでしまったわたしは、自分がどこにも存在しないような皮膚感覚にさらされている。なにしろ、わたしが行ってみたいと思っていたある特定の町に到着したわけではなく、わたしの「行きたい」という気持ちそのものが、ひとつの町である振りをしているのに騙されて、その中に迷い込んでしまったのだから。「行ってみたい」と言うからには、旅仕度をした人間がいなければいけないのに、わたしという人間はもういない。

六 憧れに向かって、百も千もの言葉を吐き出したいと思っても、言葉は出てこない。そんな時に、紙幣がオブラートのように壁や床に張り付いていることに気がついた。お札があまり薄いので、みんな気がつかないらしい。わたしは、それを一枚また一枚と剥がし始める。一枚剥がすと、その隣にもまだある。それを剥がすと更にもっとたくさん見えてくる。剥がしたお札は全部わたしのものなのだ。わたしは興奮している。そのお金は見たこともないどこかの国のお札で、もしかしたらもう存在しない国のものかもしれず、そうだとしたら使えないのだが、わたしはもともとそれを使うつもりなどない。ただ、お札がいくらでもあって、それをこのように自分だけが苦もなく集めていくことができるということが、たまらなく愉快なのだ。見上げると、それは黒い石が金の飾りをまとった巨大な寺院で、ネクタイをしめた男たちが働いている。彼等のワイシャツは、大理石でできている。これは宗教なのだ、と思うと、お札を剥がして集めるのがつまらなくなった。気がつくと、わたしは街路樹の下のベンチにすわって、路面電車の通り過ぎて行くのを眺めているのだった。

七 Zでは、それが憧れの町というだけで、どの通りの名前も意味のあるものに思えてくる。通りの名前は便利だからつけられているのだとは思わない。通りの名前などなくても、人は友達の家を見つけることはできるし、郵便配達人は手紙を配達してくれるだろう。通りの名前が何のためにあるのかは分からないけれども、とにかくそこを歩く人の気持ちを二重にする。ライオン通りを歩いていると、ライオンとは何の関係もないわたしは、ライオンは空腹でない時には鹿を襲わないとか、雌が餌を捕ってくる間、雄は昼寝をしているとか、そういう話を思い出さずにいることができない。自分もそうだろうか、自分は違うだろうか、とライオンと自分を比べる。自分の歩いている道に、必ず名称が配給されているということに、わたしは安心感を覚える。わたしは、文字というものに何よりも親しみを覚える。しかもそれは、憧れという町の通りの名前ばかりであるから、それを覚えていけば、憧れの中を溺れずに泳ぐ技術が身に付くような気がする。わたしには道順というものがなかなか覚えられない。道に迷うことなど、別に怖いとも思わない。むしろ、道に迷えば迷うほど、Zに浸る時間は長くなるわけだから、その方がいい、とさえ思う。

八　ところで、わたしがそういう駅で、通りの名前を使って作ったのは、次のような歌だった。「町は、守ってくれようとした、父親ライオンのように、でも、わたしの探すのは女神ウラニア、星座の詩神、走って行こうか、ペリカンが飛び立つ前に、ああもう遅い、将官が財布を閉めて、真っ青になって、それから、湖に飛び込んだ」。

九　歌を忘れれば、道は分からなくなる。歌を忘れても、甘いものを食べれば記憶はもどるのだと言う人もいる。わたしの持っていた聖書のような本はいつの間にか消えていた。消えたと思ったら、包み紙に包まれて、路面電車の停留所のベンチの上にあった。聖書が入っているのだろうと思って、包み紙を破いて開くと、それはホワイトチョコレートだった。わたしは、いつの間にか店の中に立っていて、まだ料金を払っていないチョコレートを裸にして、もう前歯の跡を付けてしまっていた。恥ずかしいけれどもそこで赤くなったら、みんなわたしの罪に気がついて、非難し始めるだろう。わたしは、少しも恥ずかしいことなどしていない人のように、堂々と振る舞うしかない。そうだ、わたしは、憧れの中にいるのだから、やってみたいことは何でもやっていいんだ。店の中は、菓子を包むセロハンやリボンが光を反射して奇麗で、急に涙が出そうになった。客たちはわたしが店の中で、銀色の包み紙を恥じる様子もなくむしって、平気でホワイトチョコレートを食べているので、あきれて言葉をさがしていた。みんなの常識に反することをすると、途端にみんなの目に見えてしまうらしい。そこで、わたしは自分には人に隠さなければならないようなことは何もないのだと主張するために、わざと大きめの声で、「チョコレートが甘いというのは間違えで、チョコレートは食べた瞬間、かすかに塩の味がするのに、それが反転することなく、いつの間にか砂糖の味になっているところが面白いです」と発言した。すると、そこにいた人達は、みんな顔を背けて、店を出ていった。

わたしは、Ｚにいるというだけで、憧れで喉が詰まって、ものが食べられないような気がしていたのに、そのように大きなチョコレートの塊を手に入れてしまったので困惑していた。欲しいものを欲しいと思うよりも早く、欲しい気持ちが手の形になって、それを奪ってしまう。それはだから、わたしの腕ではないのだけれど、そんなことを言っても聞いてもらえない。それから、わたしは腕時計を手にしていた。時刻が知りたかったのではない。この町では、時間は先へ進まないので、時刻なんてどうでもいい。時計を盗んでしまったのは、ショーウインドウにギリシャ語アルファベットの最後の文字「オメガ」が書いてあったからだ。Ｚもアルファベットの最後の文字だけれども、ギリシャ語の最後の文字というのが、どうしても欲しくなってしまった。わたしは盗人として、駅前通りを歩いていくことになった。わたしは水のある方向へ歩いて行けば、それで救われるのだろうと思った。水の表面が広がっている光景、それはもう町ではない。それは、自由意志で無理やり来させられた町ではない。その町自身がひそかに夢見る水の風景だ。

二一　ヨットのマストが見える。わたしはすぐそこにある湖に行き着くことができない。広場が、わたしと水を隔てている。あらゆる方向からやってきた路面電車という思考が回路を変更しながら走っていく、その広場をわたしは横断することができない。車輪たちはわたしを轢き殺そうとしている。あの線が走り去り、この線が来る前ならば、渡れるはず、などと計算してみるのだが、やっぱり渡れない。何度も最初の一歩を踏み出してみたが、それ以上、先に進むことができない。そこを渡れば、レミ通りの入り口に入ることができ、後はその管をぐっと上り詰めれば、それで満足できるのだ、と想像してみる。

二二　渡れないのならば仕方ない。諦めて、別の道を探そう。この通りを戻って、それから右手に現われるだろうリマト川を渡って、道があってもなくても、坂を上がって行こう、と決心した。しかし、夢の地形は意地悪で、よじれ、とぎれ、とける。しかも、これは夢でさえなく、わたしは目が覚めてしまっているのだった。

二三　坂を上り始めれば、呼吸が早くなるから、物の考え方も変ってくるわたしはＺがあってもなくても関係ない、という気になってくる。それどころか、わたしはこの焦げる痛さに反応して足を動かしているだけで、Ｚでは何も探していないし、このように町に包まれて幸福だ、と繰り返し自分に言ってきかせるのは、実は自分が町を壊したい、と思っているのを認めるのが怖いからなのだ、というようなことが分かってきてしまった。Ｚを破壊したい。Ｚを壊さなければ、日が暮れて星が汗のように現われても、いつまでもその中を歩き回っていなければならない。逆に、Ｚを壊してしまえば、わたしを動かすエネルギーの源が絶えてしまうから、歩けなくなってしまうかもしれない。

それとも、その時には、また別の覚醒がわたしを救ってくれるのだろうか。

# 友よ

林　京子

一 なしてか、この日は暑かとさ、と坂の下まで見送ってきた母が言った。坂の下には、光が溜るのだろうか。立っていると素肌や肩や足に、暑さがささってくる。

二 母が長崎市内に住むようになってから、二十七年が過ぎている。二十七回迎えた八月九日は、記憶にある限り、いつでも暑い、という。夏のまっ盛りだから、暑いのがあたりまえだが、母の八月九日にも、私が受けた閃光の熱さが重なってくるのだろう。

三 だけど、いい気持ちよ、と空車を探しながら私は言った。被爆してから三十二年間に、私が長崎で迎える八月九日は、これで二回目である。学生時代の夏休みにも、長崎を離れて生活をするようになってからも、八月の長崎に足を踏み入れることを、私は意識して避けてきた。長崎の、明るすぎる夏の光が、私は怖かったのである。しかし、こうして、まともに光をあびてみると、太陽がいくら暑く照りつけていても、自然の光は柔らかく、心地がよかった。

四 傘か帽子はいらんと、と母が、玄関を出るときから言っている同じ言葉を、繰り返して言った。リボンがついたピケ帽?と私は笑って言った。私たち姉妹が小学生のころ、夏になると母は必ず、可愛らしくみえるから、と言って、白いピケ帽をかぶせた。パブリックスクールの西洋人の子供たちがピケの帽子をかぶっているのをみて、母は、同じ帽子を娘たちにもかぶせてみたかったらしい。母も思い出して、ばってん、式はなんかよ、校庭であっとやろ、と笑って言った。それから、中田さんていう人の顔は覚えとるね、と聞いた。中田和子とは、N高女を卒業してから、はじめて逢うのである。三十年ぶりになる。

あんたが死んどれば、今日は三十三回忌たいね、と母が言った。

五 中田との待ち合せの時間は、八時である。城山小学校の正門に、八時までに着かなければならない。城山小学校で行われる原爆死亡者の追悼式典は、八時十分からはじまる。はじまる前に中田と逢って、お悔やみを言いたい。中田の夫は、一年前に病死している。

六 行き先と待ち合わせの時間を運転手に告げて、私はタクシーに乗った。まだ二十分はありますもんね、出勤時間ばってん何とか行けるでしょう、と運転手が言った。

七 母が住んでいる坂の上の町も、城山小学校がある浦上川沿いの城山の街も、かつての爆心地から半径一キロメートル以内にある。中田や私が被爆した兵器工場は、円内からややはずれた一・四キロメートルの地点にあたるが、城山小学校に行くためには、その前を通るはずだ。兵器工場の前を通りますか、と私は、運転手に聞いてみた。

八 兵器工場って、むかしのですか、と運転手が言った。ええ昔の、と答えてから、私は、まあ、むかしになるかしら、と言いなおした。話には聞きますばってんね、と運転手が言った。戦争が終わってから生まれたらしい運転手は、どの辺りが兵器工場の跡なのか、わからない、と言った。

九 走っているタクシーの左側に、金毘羅山の山並みが見えている。金毘羅山は、あの日に私が逃げて行った山である。長崎市内を縦走する四百メートルたらずの山だが、兵器工場を逃げ出して金毘羅山に行くまでに、私は、巾の広い川を渡った。川には、コンクリートの堰が築いてあった。たんぼに水をひくための堰で、私は、堰の上をはだしで渡った。

一〇 逃げる途中でぬげたのか、堰を渡るときにぬいだのか、私は、片方だけの下駄をさげて、水苔が生えている堰を歩いた。流れを止められた水面が盛り上がって、落差がついた川床に、白いしぶきになって散っていたのを、覚えている。街の様子は変わってしまっているが、川の流れまでは変えられないだろう。あのときの川が見つかれば、兵器工場の跡は見当がつく。私は、道の両側に川を探した。川は、見あたらず、コンクリートで塗り固められた道が、光を照り返して真っ直に続いている。坂の多い長崎の街にしては、珍しい直線の道である。

一一 十分ほど走ったころ、道は少しばかり上り坂になった。ゆるい坂を上って、下った坂の下に踏切りがあった。踏切りと、タクシーが走っている道路とは十字に交っている。城山小学校は踏切をつっ切って五、六分走ったあたりらしいが、この踏切りに、私は見覚えがあった。遮断機が降りている踏切りの際に、一間巾の狭いホームがある。ホームには、巾に見あったトタン板の屋根がついており、緑色のペンキを塗ったベンチが一つ置いてある。向かいあったホームに、出勤するサラリーマンたちが乗物を待っている。

一二 乗物が市電なのかバスなのか、あるいは諫早に通じている国鉄の汽車なのか、私には判断がつかなかった。赤錆びたレールが敷かれているから、バスの路線ではないようだが、それにしてはレールが錆びついている。

一三 ただ、私の記憶が正しいならば、それは市電のホームで、かつて私が学徒のころ、兵器工場に通うために利用していた、大橋の停留所のはずである。そのころは大橋の停留所が終点で、それから先の兵器工場までの道を、学徒も工員も、列をなして歩いていた。終点の停留所から工場の正門までは、歩いて十分はかかったが、いま見ると、停留所の先が踏切りになっていて、線路らしきものが延びて行っている。

一四 ここは大橋の停留所でしょう、と私は運転手に尋ねてみた。よう知っとんなるですね、と運転手が言った。

一五 終点じゃなかった？と私は聞いた。いまはアカサコまで行っとりますよ、と私の知らない土地の名前を、運転手が言った。私は、腕の時計を見た。八時に七、八分前である。

一六 昭和二十年の八月九日の、ちょうど同じ時刻ごろ、私はこのホームで市電をおりた。あの日の朝も、今日のようによく晴れていた。

そして今日まで、一度も私はこの場所へきたことがない。

一七 ホームの屋根のトタン板が腐蝕して、穴があいている。小さな、針でつついたような無数の穴から光が抜けて、ホームを歩く人たちの頭髪や、白いワイシャツの背中で蜂の巣のように、揺れ動いている。出勤時の風景は、三十二年前の朝と変りがなかった。遮断機が上るのを待っているタクシーの中から、私はホームの風景を眺めていた。私は、自分一人が年を経て、三十二年前の風景を眺めている、奇妙な錯覚に襲われた。真夏の外気から隔絶された、タクシーの冷房のせいだろうか。それとも、思いが切実に重ならない違和感は、私の中でも八月九日は遠い昔になってしまったせいだろうか。

一八　約束の時間きっかりに、タクシーは城山小学校に着いた。城山小学校は、中田の出身校である。戦時中の卒業生だから、当時の城山国民学校になる。記録によると八月九日の当日、学校には百五十一名の人たちがいた。兵器工場から分散されてきていた学徒や、城山国民学校の教職員たちである。そのうちの百三十一名が死亡している。中田の恩師たちは、殆どが即死している。

一九　中田は、恩師たちの慰霊のために毎年、欠かさずに追悼式に出席していた。小学校での追悼式典が終わると、歩いて二十分ばかりで行ける爆心地の平和公園に行き、十一時二分の、原爆炸裂時刻の黙とうを捧げる。これが中田の例年のしきたりになっている。長崎で生活をしていない私は、今日一日を中田の行動に従うつもりでいた。

二〇　現在の城山小学校は、全壊した校舎の跡地に建てられたものである。小高い丘になっていて、正門までには五十段はある石段をの上らなくてはならない。私は、指示されたように石段を上った。中田らしき人影は見あたらなかった。私は、石の間柱のまん前に立って中田を待った。

二一　追悼式に出席する児童たちが、石段を上ってくる。夏休みなので、出席する子供たちは三年生以上の高学年生に限られているようだ。半ズボンや、短いスカートの裾から伸びた足は、しっかりと肉がしまっていて、首筋や肩が、茶褐色に日焼けしている。長崎の街は海に近いせいか、子供たちは夏休みじゅう海に行って遊んでいる。

二二　石段を上りきった校舎の正面に、少年の立像があった。左の腕に一羽のハトを止まらせたブロンズの像は、「少年平和像」と呼ばれて、被爆死した児童たちの供養の像である。四、五人の子供たちが、報道関係のカメラマンの注文に応じて、黄色と白との菊の花束を少年に捧げ、両手を合せて黙とうをしている。毎年のことなのだろう。子供たちは写されるのに慣れていて、カメラの前で、素直に感情を出して祈っている。

二三 ベルが鳴った。追悼式典がはじまる合図のベルである。式は、炎天下の校庭をさけて、講堂で行われるようだ。児童や、喪服を着た大人たちが、別棟になっている講堂に入って行く。ベルの音を聞いて、数人の子供たちが石段を駈け上ってくる。その中に、白地に黒い線描き模様の、絹地のワンピースを着た中年の女がいる。小刻みに、つま先で駈け上ってくる足の運び具合も、石段を見あげて、誰かを探しているらしい丸い、黒い目の動きも、少女のころの中田に似ている。

二四 三十年ぶりの再会でありながら、私たちは、おたがい確かめあう必要はなかった。待った?と中田が息をはずませて聞いた。左の唇の端の傷が、話しかけるときに、僅かにひきつった。八月九日に受けたガラス片の傷跡は、知っている者が注意をして見なければわからないほどに、薄くなっている。待った、と私は冗談を言った。

二五 私たちは、スリッパにはきかえて、講堂に入った。小学生たちは既に整列して、式典のはじまりを待っている。子供たちを囲むまわりの壁には、被爆直後の写真が展示してあり、列の後には、椅子が並べてある。遺族席なのか、喪服を着た大人たちが坐っている。

二六 城山小学校の、被爆死した百三十一名の中には児童は数えられていない。夏休み中だったので、子供たちは自宅にいた。千四百名にのぼる子供たちは、自宅で被爆死している。親も子も、一家全滅の地域だから、喪服の大人たちが遺族だとすれば、奇蹟的に助かった人たちだ。

二七 私は、椅子が置いてある場所をさけて、入口に近い壁ぎわに立って式典を待った。中田も私と並んで立った。

テレビカメラが入っているので、子供たちは行儀がよかった。おしゃべりをしている子供は見あたらない。私が小学生のころは、式がはじまる前には、鼻をすすりあげる音が講堂一杯に響きわたったが、鼻をすすりあげる者もいない。しかし、人目につかない場所で子供たちは、やはりいたずらをしていた。後から二、三番目に立っている二人の少女が、袖なしの、ワンピースから出ている肩と肩をくっつけて、どっちの肌が日に焼けているか、比べあっている。見比べているうちに、一人の女の子が、相手の肩先に日焼けして、皮がむけているのを見つけたらしい。首だけを真横にねじって、相手の肩の皮を、爪の先ではがしはじめた。皮をむかれている女の子も、自分の肩や腕の、皮がむけかけた箇所を探している。皮をむいたり、見比べている子供たちの動作を眺めているうちに、私は、八月九日の自分の姿を思い出した。あの日、焼け野原に立って、私は腕をなで、肩をなで、そっと頬を撫でてみた。火傷もなく、皮がむけていないのを確かめると、私は一目散に金毘羅山に向かって走った。

二八 両腕の皮が、湯びきのように白く縮まって垂れさがっている中学生が、痛か、いたか、と独り言を言って、目の前を逃げて行った。

二九 三十二年を経過した光景には、比べようのない開きがあったが、かげりのない子供たちの動作を見ても、ことさらな、平和への感慨はわかなかった。あの日と今日とが二つ並んで、平面な、対等な位置で私の内にあった。あるがままを受け入れて生きることに慣らされたせいか、八月九日にも、平和な今日にも、私の意識は鈍になりつつあるようだった。

三〇 中田も、子供たちの様子に気がついていた。私たちは顔を見あわせて、微かに笑った。意味のない笑いだったが、中田は優しい目をしていた。中田の黒く大きな目は、少女のころにはもっと険があったはずだ。

三一　式がはじまるまでに二、三分の間があった。私は辺りに聞こえないように、ご主人、大変だったのね、と悔みを言った。中田は、う？と短く言葉を切った。暫く間をおいてから、人が死ぬことには慣れているから、おたがいに、ね、と言った。少女のころよりも低い声で話す中田の言葉を、死者を大勢みてきた被爆者同士の、儀礼的な挨拶だと私は思った。

三二　淋しいでしょうけど、頑張ってね、と私は言った。中田は、ううん、と静かな声で、しかし頑固に否定した。そして、人の命を数で比較するわけじゃないけど、六人も死んでいるから、と標準語で言った。

三三　ええ、と私は聞き返した。六人も死んでいるから、と言う言葉の意味が、私には理解できなかったのである。

三四　知らんやったと、と中田が聞いた。知らない、と私は答えた。あのころ、あたしは話さんやったもんね、母と姉たちが死んだとよ、家が城山にあったろうが、と言った。私は茫然として中田の顔を見た。

三五　開会の辞を、男の教師が告げた。黒いレースの喪服を着た、恰幅のいい女性が壇上に立って一礼をした。校長先生よ、と中田が教えてくれた。ライトが校長の顔面を照らして、テレビカメラが廻りはじめた。

三六　中田は、水晶の数珠を左手にかけて、一つ一つの珠を指先でさぐりながら、校長の話を聞いている。珠と珠がふれあって鳴る硬質な音を聞きながら、私は、中田の言葉を思っていた。

三七　戦争が終わって、二学期の授業が十月から開始されると、長崎で家を焼かれた女学生たちは、近郊の市や村の疎開先から、汽車通学をはじめた。その中の一人に中田がいた。中田は、私と同じ諫早から通学をしていた。

三八　中田の家は、本明川の流れに沿った県道筋にあって、二階建ての、風呂屋のように大きな家だった。諫早駅の近くにあり、私は、通りすがりに毎朝声をかけた。当時、私たちは六時九分発の列車に乗っていた。冬などは、まだまっ暗である。外灯も、人通りもない道を一人で歩いていると、本明川の、さわさわと流れる水音が聞こえる。その水音が、人が、群がってついてくる足音に聞こえて、私は足を早める。怖さが達したころに、中田の家の灯りが見える。私は、大声で中田を呼んだ。台所の隣の部屋に灯りがついていて、声をかけると、女のひとが返事をする。

三九　灯りの中でオカッパの頭が揺れて、下駄音をたてて中田が出てくる。白い、木綿のハンカチに包んだ平べったい弁当箱をカバンと一緒に右手にさげて、駈け出してくる。女のひとの声の調子や、灯りの落ちつき具合からみると、声をかけるのを待っている様子なのに、いつも決まって、慌てて出てきた。

四〇　六時九分発の列車は、門司港から下ってくる夜行列車だったと思う。闇物資の買い出し客が多く、列車はいつも満員である。座席に坐れることはまずない。乗り損なわないように、敏捷に行動するのが先決で、私たちはホームを走って、比較的空いている列車をみつけて乗る。空いている列車は決っていて、前から三輛目の列車によく乗った。浦上の家を焼かれて、大草から通学をはじめた島も、三輛目の列車に乗ってきた。

四一　そのころ、私たちは三年生だったのだろうか。それとも四年生に進級した、一学期の冬だったのだろうか。寒い季節だった。

四二　ある朝、私たちは、将来結婚をするか、独身を通すかという話をはじめた。中田と私と、大草から乗ってきた島と、他に二、三人の同学年生がいたようだ。結婚するやろうね、と漠然と二、三人の者が認めて言った。中田と島の二人は黙っていた。私は、あなたも結婚するわよね、と中田に言った。中田は首をかしげて考えていたが、わたしはせんよ、と言った。うそ、と誰かが言下に否定した。

四三　嘘じゃなかよ、と中田が言った。

結婚をしてもしなくとも、私たちは、どっちでもよかったのである。ただ、結婚という未知な将来について、夢をまじえながら希望を話しあいたい、浮きたった話題が欲しかったのである。それを中田から、はっきり否定されると、私たちは面白くなかった。

四四 なぜさ、理由言ってよ、一生涯？と矢つぎ早に質問をした。中田は質問には答えないで、あたしは結婚せんよ、と言い張った。ほんとうに？と私たちは、しつこく聞いた。

四五 本当さ、と中田も繰り返して答えた。何とか本心を聞き出そうと、言葉をかえて誘いをかける私たちに、中田の答えは変わらなかった。へえーと私たちは、声を揃えて大げさに驚いてみせた。周りに立っている乗客たちが私たちを見たが、気にとめなかった。

わけを話してよ、と言った。中田は唇をかんで、取り囲んでいる一人一人を見ていた。

四六 中田は、頭がいい女学生である。同学年生の中に人気があって、学生を代表する行事には必ず選び出される。各課目が、むらなくできる中田に勝てる者は、汽車通学生の中にはいない。ただ中田のように優等生タイプの少女には、何処か、いじめたくなる要素がある。それは中田自身が持っている性格よりも、むしろ、いじめる側にいる、あまり出来のよくない私たちの方にあるのかも知れなかった。

四七 中田は、珍しくむきになっていた。相手が真剣になればなるだけ、私たちは意地が悪くなった。中田は、我慢ができなくなったのだろう。かみしめていた唇を開いて、トラピストに言って修道女になるのよ、と強い口調で言った。女学生らしい、優等生らしい答えだった。純粋な少女期には、誰もが一応考えることだが、結婚する、と答えた私たちにとっては、癇にさわる答えである。いい子でありすぎる。

四八 中田は、結構いたずらをする。汽車通学をしている男子学生の名前もよく知っていて、品定めをする。ばたばたと慌てる面を持っていながら、根気よく、空きそうな席をみつけて、一人だけ坐ってにこにこしている。それに、くりくりよく動く大きな目は、男子学生たちに人気があった。

四九 トラピストだって、あなたが、と私たち言った。行くつもりでいる、と言う中田の言葉を、片っぱしから否定していった。中田はとうとう黙った。目の玉から涙がこぼれ落ちた。中田は顔を伏せないで、大きな目を見開いて泣いていた。涙をみて、私たちは、はじめて責めるのを止めた。泣かしてしまった後悔と、泣かしてしまった満足感が交差してあった。

五〇 六人も死んでいるから、という中田の言葉を耳にした瞬間に私が絶句したのは、終戦直後の、汽車の中の情景が浮かんだからである。

五一 涙をこぼしながら、最後まで声をたてなかった中田の表情と共に、泣くまで追い詰めたあの時の言葉の数数が、鮮やかに、記憶の底から盛りあがってきた。かたくなに結婚を拒否して、トラピストの修道女になるといい切った中田の心のうちには、被爆死した母や姉たちへの、供養の気持があったはずである。断ちきれない愛しさがあったはずである。

五二 一瞬の間に、外地にいる父親だけを残して、肉親の全員を亡くした中田の悲しみは、私には察しようがない。悲しみのやり場もない中田は、修道女になろうと思いつめていたのだろう。何よりも、自分自身の悲しみから中田は救われたかったのだろう。

そんな中田を、私たちは責めた。

五三 灯りがついた部屋から返事をしていた女のひとを、私は、中田の母親だと思っていたが、そうではなかったのだ。

五四 校長の訓辞は、まだ続いていた。私は、知らなかったのよ、ほんとうに、と心の中でつぶやいた。女学生の、他愛のない意地悪だったのだ、とも弁解してみた。しかし弁解は弁解でしかなかった。悔は年月の経過を飛び越して、私を、いたたまれない気持に追い込んだ。

五五 私は、列車の中での会話を私たちを書いたが、どれほど大勢の人間があの場にいあわせていたとしても、私が言った言葉の重さには変りがない。結婚とか恋愛の話になると、誰よりも多弁になる島が、あのときは、全く口をはさまなかった。ね？と誘っても、島は話には加わらなかった。島も、母親と祖父母を浦上で亡くしているが、だからなのだろう、という島への配慮さえも私にはなかった。

五六 中田も島も、そして私も被爆者である。私は、被爆者の不幸を、八月九日の共通の日に立って、同じ被爆者として苦しんできたつもりでいた。しかし、私はあの日に、家族の、誰ひとりも亡くしてはいない。私は、彼女たちの何を知り、何を理解したつもりで今日まで生きてきたのだろうか。

五七 追悼式は終わった。中田が、ちょっと坐らん、と椅子を指して言った。私は、中田の後について椅子に坐った。知らなかったのよ、と私は歯切れの悪い言葉遣いで言った。なんのこと、と中田が聞いた。式典の前の、短い会話を忘れてしまって中田は聞き返したのだろうが、私には痛い質問だった。

五八 お母さまたちのこと、と私は言った。ああ、と中田は思い出して、よかとよ、知らんとはあなただけじゃなかし、話せば泣きとうなるけん、あのころは一生懸命頑張っとったさ、と言った。ごめんなさいね、と私は頭を下げた。中田が驚いた表情で、なにを謝ると、と聞いた。汽車通学のころのこと、と私は言った。中田は笑った。忘れとった、と言って中田は笑った。

五九 小学生のころから修道女になりたかったとよ、と中田は言った。城山町にあった中田の家から、浦上の天主堂は近く、子供のころ、よく天主堂に行って遊んでいたという。

六〇 冬になると修堂女たちは、葡萄酒色の修道服を着る。葡萄酒色の修道婦服を着た修道女たちが、活発な足どりで天主堂の坂道を降りてくる。褐色に冬枯れした石垣の草や、柔らいだ光に似合っていて美しい。あこがれとったっさ、と中田は言った。

トラピストにも行かんやったし、独身も通さんやったし、と中田は言って笑った。

六一 児童たちは退場してしまっていた。講堂には五、六人の大人たちが残って、壁に展示してある写真を眺めている。写真は、八月九日の被爆直後から、十月までの浦上を写した写真である。

六二 報道写真家が撮影したフィルムで、進駐軍の命令で発表が禁じられていた貴重な写真である。中田と私は椅子を立って、百枚ほど展示してある写真の一つ一つを、見て廻った。二人が学徒動員で働いていた兵器工場の写真が数点あった。

六三 説明文と写真を読み比べていくうちに、中田が、一枚の写真の前で立ち止った。顔を写真につけて、画面を試すように見ている。中田の肩越しに見ると、向き合った白い壁が二枚、ガレキの中に焼け残っている写真である。

六四 爆心地に向いた二面の壁と、屋根が吹き飛んでいて、両側の二面の壁だけが残った写真である。閃光と、爆風の特徴が如実に現われた破壊現場の写真として、私は二、三回同じ写真を見ていた。白壁の家は、どこかの大学の研究所に使われていたらしい。

六五 どうしたの、と私は中田に聞いた。中田は黙って、白い壁と、説明文を指した。そして、「うちが燃えてる」と震える声で言った。見ると、白い壁の後方に、白い煙が昇っている。中田がいう、「家」はみあたらないが、確かに、何かが燃えている。それを中田は、あたしのうち、と指をさして言った。

六六 中田は両手で口を押えると、声をころして泣いた。肩をしぼめて、しっかりと唇を押さえている指の間から、嗚咽がもれた。それは悲鳴だった。

六七 中田の家は、白壁の研究所の真裏にあったという。印刷業をしていて、紙や油があったので火勢はひどく、中田の叔父たちが焼け跡に遺体を探しに行ったが、近づけなかった。

六八 火は数日間燃え続け、まだ煙が立っている焼け跡から、中田の母と姉たちの骨を、叔父が拾って諫早に帰ってきた。

六九 兵器工場で被爆した中田は、工場の鉄骨の下で夕暮になるまで意識をなくして、倒れていた。助け出されて、汽車に乗せられて、そのまま、諫早よりも先の大村まで運ばれている。

七〇 中田は、私のように焼け跡から逃げていないから、被爆地の煙や焼け跡の状況は見ていない。中田もまだ、今日まで、家の焼け跡を訪ねたことはないという。

写真は、中田がはじめて目にする、我が家の焼け跡だった。煙だった。

七一 写真は中田の目前で、白い煙をあげて燃えていた。中田に向かって言うべき言葉は、私にはなかった。私は、泣いている中田の横に立っていた。

# 草木

中上健次

山中で男に会った。あと小一時間も歩けば、大台ヶ原に行きつく、山の中腹あたりだった。杉の根方に背をあててしゃがみ込み、肩で荒い息をしていた。左脚のふともも、ふくらはぎに、折れた矢がくい込み、血を流していた。男は、彼をみた。ずっと以前から、彼が歩いてくるのを知っていたらしかった。身を隠すにも、もう身動きがとれない様子だった。最初、その男を、この熊野山中に棲む神か、と思った。ここには一本足の、つまり片方の足の機能を損じたイッポンダタラと称せられる大きな神がいた。男は神ではなかった。ただ片方の眼が、血膿で固っていた。「どうしたのですか？」彼は男の前に立って訊いた。男は黙って首を振った。彼は、幻だろうと思った。山中で、よく人は、死んだ近親の者、縁あってなお遠く離れているものの姿をみた。彼もみた。じいんじいんと蝉の声がするだけになった自分の体のすぐかたわらを、近親の者は、通り過ぎた。それこそ魂の幻なのだろうと彼は思った。

[二]「どうしたのですか?」彼はまた訊いた。

「故あって傷つき申した」男は唸るように言った。彼をにらみつけた。下手なことをすると、喉元を噛みちぎるという構えだった。彼は、男の前に屈み、腰につるした水瓶を差し出した。男は彼の顔をみつめながら、それをひったくった。キルクの蓋を歯で開けて飲んだ。唇からあふれこぼれた水は男のあごを濡らし、首筋を伝い、破れて土埃でよごれた衣服に流れおちた。短かい毛の生えた胸に、水がゆっくり流れ落ちるのが、破れ目からみえた。いや、破れ目ではなかった。厚い生地の服を柔道着のように前をあわせて着ていた。なにやら奇妙な生き物に思えた。人ともけものとも判別がつかない。男は空になるまで飲みつくし、そしてやっと水瓶を返した。男は深く息を吐いた。立ちあがろうとした。よろけた。思わず踏みしめた左脚から血が流れ出した。男は杉の木に背をかけて、立った。上背が彼をしのいだ。蝉の声が、遠くで聞こえた。杉木立の湿ったにおいがした。

[三]「敗れてしもうた」男は杉の木に手をかけて、傷ついた自分の体をふがいないというように、言った。水瓶を差し出すと言葉遣いは変っていた。左眼が潰れているのが、納得できないと首を振り、手で押えた。「ものの見事に、やられた。敗れたら、しまいじゃ。やられた、やられた」男は言った。わらった。

「どこへ行くのですか?」彼は訊いた。「伊勢の方へ行くのですか、熊野の村の方へおりるのですか?」

[四]「わしに行くところがどこにあろかよ。どこにもありやせん。いや、いや」と男はまた首を振った。「どこであろと、のう、落ちてゆくわい。どこへでも行くわい」男は一歩踏み出し、次の一歩が出ず、よろけてしまった。彼は、男を支えようと思って、手を差し出した。男は、激しく振り払った。男は尻餅をついた。杉の木に頭を打ちつけた。それでも彼は男にむかって手を出し、男の腰をかかえあげた。今度は、拒まなかった。腕を、

彼の肩にあげてそれで男の体重を支えた。けもののにおいがした。それは人間本来のにおいなのだろう、彼が仕事場で貨物に足をやられてしばらく入院していた時、洗わない頭、股間からけもののにおいが立った。男を支えて、杉木立の中を歩いた。すぐ、崖っぷちに出た。白く明るい日が、崖の草木の緑を照らしていた。男の口から息がもれるたびにシュッシュッと音がした。男を岩においた。男は彼の顔をみつめ、それから、「ここに置いて先を行って下され」と言った。一羽、崖の下から、鴉がとびあがった。「それとも、いっそ、のう、ここから下へ放り込んでくれんか？」男は、唇を閉じた。そうやって自力で歩くこともできない自分が、よほどふがいないのか、と彼は思った。そこから山々のつらなりがみえた。果しがなかった。鴉が五羽、また下方から舞いあがってきた。湯の出る所まで二つほど山を越えなければならないはずだった。思案する時間を与えると、男は、山中で行き会った見知らぬ人間に救けられる心苦しさがわきあがるのだろうと、彼は、「さあ、行きますか」と声を掛けた。男を抱えた。二人で、よろぼいながら、崖のふちに残った道を降りた。またすぐに丈高い杉木立に入った。道は、崖をはずれた。耳に、蝉の声と、それにあわせてたてる男と彼の、息の音がした。男はしきりに右手で左眼をこすっていた。ふっと、彼は、東京に残してきた小鳥のことを想った。あれこそ、幻かもしれない。

五

兄の法事で熊野に来る直前に、気づいたのだった。この春に巣立ちした十姉妹の一羽が盲いていた。原因は何によるのかわからなかった。巣立ちの頃に栄養が欠けたためか、それとも遺伝子の悪戯で、たまたま劣性がかけ合うことになったためか。純白の羽毛だった。親の種鳥は、並の、つまり白黒のまだらだった。檀特からいま十姉妹に変異したというような健康なやつだった。近親交配のせいか、と思った。デパートの小鳥屋で買ったものだった。一つの店で雌雄を買うと、よく兄妹をつかまされる。いやな気がした。どうしようか、と思った。相手は人間ではなく、小鳥だ。盲いて生れた小鳥など、飼っていても、苦しくなるだけだ。元々、十姉妹など姿形を楽しむものでもないし、声を賞でるものでもない。健康にピッピッと鳴きとびはね、少々の乱暴も気にかけず、巣があれば卵を産み、雛を育て、巣立ちすれば三ヵ月ほどで一人前になる、という雑草のたくましさが身上だ。いっそ殺してしまおうか？彼は金網にとまったままの十姉妹を、つついた。指が、嘴に触ると、すぐ逃げた。合計十姉妹だけで何羽いるのだろうか、一メートル四方の十姉妹専用の雑居籠の留り木は、うずめつくされていた。盲目の十姉妹は、その中に割り込めず、すとんと下に落ち、うまい具合に餌台に立つ。瞳孔のあたりが白く濁っている。

六

きれいな十姉妹だった。また金網にとまる。なにをみているのか、ぼんやりとしている。そのうち、体のむきを変え、とびおりる。餌台におりて、餌をついばむ。水を飲む。また金網にとまる。そのくり返しだった。殺してやろうと思いつづけたのだった。いっそこの世に生命を受けたことなど、なかったことにしろ。手を籠の中に差し入れる。十姉妹どもは騒いでまわった。金網に体をぶつけた。籠の三方をおおった板に体当りして下に落ちた。巣の後に隠れるものもあった。盲いた十姉妹は、籠の隅で、首をのばして立ち、いつでもとびあがれる姿勢を取っていた。彼の大きな手が、つかんだ。それではじめて、自分がわけの分からないとてつもなく大きなものにつかまえられたと気づいたふうに、翼をふる。もがく。逃げ出そうとする。日が当っていた。彼は、力を入れた。純白の羽毛の十姉妹はもがいた。そのまま力を入れれば、柔らかい骨の小鳥は潰れて死ぬはずだった。いつかも、そんなふうにして殺した。それはセキセイインコだった。買ってきても買ってきても、小鳥は死んだ。朝、仕事に出かける時、あんなにも元気だった小鳥が、夕、仕事から帰ると羽毛をふくらませ、留り木にもとまれず、よろぼうていた。籠を暖め、口を開けて、薬を飲ませた。夜、枕元に置いた籠の底で、立つこともできず、ただパタパタ翼を底板に打ちつけていた。いつの間にか眠り、不意にめざめると、死んでいた。そんなことをみるに耐えず、嘔吐をくり返し、苦しみもだえる小鳥を、手で握って窒息死させた。安楽死ではなかった。ただみたくなかった。苦しむことなど知恵の備わった人間だけで充分だった。彼の手の中の十姉妹は、あまりに小さすぎた。盲いていることに、無頓着すぎた。彼は、籠の中に、もう一度十姉妹をもどした。

七　彼は大きな体の男だった。他人には、小鳥の飼育に熱中するようなタイプにみえなかった。人は、彼がその大きな武骨な手で小さな華奢な小鳥の世話をしている図は、童話の“わがままな巨人”のようだと言った。確かに巣引きをしている小鳥と、それを見守っている彼の姿は、おかしくもたのしくもある。ほのぼのともしよう。それが、死穢や奇形、変異にみまわれることがないならばだ。籠の中で、餌箱のへりに立ち、餌を食べることもなく、いつでもどこかへとびあがれるように首をのばし、翼をぴったり背にくっつけている。なにものかを念じ、呼んででもいるように、白く濁った瞳孔をこちらにむけ、盲いて生れた十姉妹はとまっている。留り木にひしめき、金網にとまった健康なやつが、その十姉妹を中心にして餌をついばみ、水を飲み、とびまわっているようにみえる。磁力をその純白の羽毛から発しているようにみえる。

八　錦華鳥を種鳥の籠と雑居籠の二つに分けていた時のことだった。雌一羽、雄四羽の雑居籠の中の巣に、卵が産まれているのを知っていたが、どうせ、と思い、ほうっておいた。臆病な鳥だった。物音ひとつしても、籠の中を大騒ぎしてとびまわった。人影をさえぎるために金網に紙を貼りつけても、せっかく長いことかかって抱いて自分でかえした雛を、物音を聞いてあわてふためき、巣から蹴りおとしたり、巣草の中に隠す。雛は死ぬ。そんなふうにした、何羽雛が死んだかわからない。まさに毛虫同然の姿だった。落ちて頭にうっすらと血をにじませて死んでいるのもいた。その雑居籠を掃除したついでに、卵をとりのぞいた。割ってみてもしないでそのまま二個、ゴミ箱にほうり込んだ。もののついでと、一つを割った。中で、赤い肉が、ひくひくと動いていた。思わず息を呑んだ。手のひらの中で、外気にさらされてもまだ小さいものの心臓の鼓動そのままに、ひく、ひく、と動いていた。殺すつもりなど毛頭なかった。これは過ちだ。過ちだ。許してくれ。彼は言った。仏か、神か、それとももっと別のものかもしらんが、赤むけのむきだしの生命にむかって、この罰当りのおれを許してくれ。日の光を、この時ほど痛く強く体に感じたことはなかった。自分生命がむきだしになり、日と空気にさらされて、じいんじいんと脈打ちうずいている。そんな風に過って卵を割ってしまったのは、四度ほどあった。そのまま孵化しても、盲いて生れるかもしれないが、「発心集」にあらわれた鷹飼いの話など、ほとんど彼と、経験を同じゅうする。母犬の裂かれた腹からみえたのは、まだ皮膚もつくることのない赤い肉の生命そのものだ。血が忌わしいのではない。肉そのものが忌わしいのではない。母の腹の暗がりの中にいて生命を形づくった、その小さいものの、無垢な、ひくひくと動く、生命そのものが、忌わしい。

九

蝉の声が幾重にも重なっていた。いや、男と彼の息の音が、まるで、耳のそばで幾千幾万の人間が、いま、息を吐き吸っているかのようにきこえた。男の体は重かった。汗が眼に膜を張っていた。彼が反対に男に抱えられ、山中を歩いているように思えた。左眼を潰され、左脚を損じたのは自分だ。杉木立が続いた。日は真上にあるのに、梢で遮られていた。盲いて生れたのはこのおれだ。まだ暗がりにいるところを、いきなり破られ、日にさらされてひくひくと動くのはこのおれだ。この肉だ。露出した岩をよけ、ふらふらと歩いた。そこから丈低い草の生えたなだらかな坂になっていた。わき水の横に男をおろした。「ここへ置いていって下され」男は言った。「どうして救けようとする？」

一〇

彼は黙って、わき水を飲み、頭をぬらし胸をぬらした。まだるっこしく、腹這いになり、頭をつっ込んだ。ひととき、我を忘れていた。なんどもなんども頭に水をかぶった。男があごをあげ、荒い息を吐いていることに気づき、水瓶に水をくみ、差し出した。男は首を振った。呻いた。腹を脈打たせていた。彼は水を男の顔にかけた。それから、彼は腰に引っかけていたタオルを取って水にひたし、男の顔をぬぐった。血膿で固まった左眼にふれぬように気をつけ、垢とも土埃ともつかぬものがこびりついた顔をふいた。たっぷり水を含ませて、男の脇の下、腹をふいてやった。「すまん」と男は言った。男は誰かに似ていると思った。思い出せなかった。タオルを水で洗いなおし、折れた矢のくい込んだところをぬぐった。矢尻が肉にのめり込み、手でつかむこともできないくらいで二つとも折れていた。すぐにも外科医にみせねば、手のほどこし様がなくなる。いったい、この男は、なにをやってきたのだろう。誰がやったのだろう。わからなかった。空で、とびが舞っていた。音はなかった。まだ一つの山を半分も越えていなかった。

一一

「さあ行くぞ」彼が言った。男を抱き起こした。拒んだ。蝉が鳴き交いはじめた。左眼が潰れ、左脚は動かない。男は、呻いた。このまま動かずに、こうした草の中にいたい。このままこうしていると、傷が化膿し、体が発熱し、吹いてくる風にさえ痛くうずき、生命は果て、腐る。鴉が体にむらがる。眼球をほじくり、腹を破り、肉を啄む。空に舞いあがる。男は、彼に支えられて立ちあがった。彼はまた、男をかかえて歩きはじめた。自分が歩いているのではなかった。形をもたない赤むけのひくひく動く肉が、もうひとつ赤むけの傷ついた肉をかかえて歩いていた。なにも考えなかった。なにも感じなかった。崖をまわり込む形で、おりた。わき出た水でこけの生えた岩をまたぎ、かすかに一本残っている道を歩いた。男は、ほとんど重さを感じなかった。二人の息の音が、彼には、以前にも増して数えきれないくらいになったのを知った。ぞろぞろ群をなして、赤むけの傷ついた肉をかかえて、肉が歩いていた。後にもいた。声がきこえた、男は呻いた。坂を降り、すぐまた木立の中にはいった。日が空でかげったらしく、光はなかった。いきなり、男が泣き出した。「ここで、殺してくれ、ねがいだ」と叫んだ。「頼む、頼む、殺してくれ」男の声は割れて笛のようにひびいた。「どこの方か存じませんが、眼一つ脚一つにされたおれを殺してくれ。首をしめてくれ。そこの杉にこの頭を打ちつけてくれえ。岩をめがけてつきおとしてくれ」男は叫んだ。男をなだめようと杉の根方に背をもたせかけ、坐らせた。色の変った左脚をのばし、右脚をたてて、バネにし、男は後頭部を杉にむかって打ちつけた。いざりより、むきを変えようとして体の平衡を失い、男は横倒しになった。「一人で死ぬこともできん」男は言った。男は口をあけた。下の歯が全部欠けているらしかった。男は涙を流した。

二二「いったい誰にやられたのですか？」彼は訊いた。男は、黙ったままだった。

彼は立っていた。横倒しになって、手で顔をおさえて、声を殺して泣く男をみていた。村の者にやられたのだろう、それとも何百年もの前の戦で敗れたのだろうか？その敗れた者の魂か？彼はわからなかった。それが現なのか幻なのかわからなかった。敗れたというのなら、彼もそうだった。やられたというのなら、彼もそうだった。大きな体の男だった。男のもらす泣き声が、山中で、何倍もの音量でひびきこもる。山全体が、敗れ、やられて、片眼、片脚になり、それでも自死すらできぬ男の、声でいっぱいになる。彼の体まで、楽器のように鳴っている。

二三 泣き続ける男のわきに坐り、杉に体をもたせかけ、しばらくその音をきいていた。梢と梢が重なり合い、震え合い、鳴るのだった。日が射さないために、ひょろひょろと柔らかに育った草が、男の声、息の音に呼応して鳴るのだった。蝉の声が、共鳴するのだった。山全体が、いま男に合わせて、泣いているのだった。彼はしばらく、そうしていたかった。そうしていると、卵を割って見つけた赤むけの肉のような彼の体が、あらたにいまいちど破け、生命の本の本が、あらわれてくる。生命の本の本、それは物も言わず、聴えず、見えず、感じもせず、考えもさせぬこの闇、その光だ。闇はいっぱいある。彼は、男の泣き声に共振れする自分の体、自分の骨に恍惚となりながら、ある日ある朝、庭の土をほじくっているとと出てきた発芽寸前のソラマメのように、手足を屈め、体をまるめていた。杉のにおいと泣き声と木立がかかえた湿気た空気の中で、自分があたうる限り小さく変化するのを知る。そして、シダの胞子さながら、吹きぬけてくる風にふうっと浮かぶ。彼は男と共に泣きながら、眠り、めざめては泣いた。おまえはあの兄か、それともあの男かと問うた。眠った。そうだ、左眼を潰し、左脚をそこない、もう自死すらできぬ具合にしたのはわれわれだ。このおれだ。だがしかし、このおれとは、なんなのだ。生命の取った形か？そして彼は、みた。山の下、熊野の母の家で、法事が行われていたのだった。なむあみだぶつ、なむあみだぶつ、なむあみだぶつ、と集まってくれた近隣の人は、和尚の声が一区切りするたびに口々の唱和した。人々は背をまるめ、身をちいさくしていた。母は和尚のすぐ後に坐っていた。ほうぼうから戻った姉たち三人はすぐ横にいた。義父と義父の子と、彼がいた。仏壇にとぼしたろうそくの火黄色く赤くみえた。いま、法事が行われている。母の家で、彼は、いっこうに有難さのわからぬ和尚の読経に耳を傾け、なむあみだぶつ、なむあみだぶつと小声で唱えている。読経がとぎれ、焼香をはじめる。そうだ、それは幻だ。この山中で男の泣き声に共振れをおこし、泣いて、眠り、めざめてはまた泣いているのが、彼だ。母は、肥りむくみ心筋硬塞の発作で黒ずんだ顔をあげ、阿弥陀如来の御名を唱え、それから、焼香する。彼は母をみている。男のことも、兄のことも、いい。自分自身のことも、いい。母をこそ、せめて自然に、草が立ち枯れるように死なせてやりたい。母は焼香を終えると、姉たちに、かすかにけむりの立つ焼香の盆をまわす。次々焼香する。彼もする。和尚の読経は続いている。突然、彼は思い出したのだった。いまの彼の齢より若い兄が、この仏壇に宗旨の違う法華経を一時間ほど唱え、よし、おれが、行く、と言い、次の日早朝くべれて死んでいたのを。自分が死ねば、すべてが治まる。それからことあるごとに、姉たち、母たちは、魂呼ばいの巫女にでもなったように兄の名を口にした。母や姉たちは、まるで盲いた十姉妹のようなものだった。それ以降、兄と彼がシャム双生児にでもなったように彼をみるたびに、兄を呼んだ。

一四　男はいた。もう泣いてはいなかった。日が、杉木立の上で、暮れかかっているらしく、寒かった。湿気が、鼻先にここちよかった。男は、杉の幹に背をもたせかけ、坐っていた。男の息の音は、静かだった。いまさっきまで、自分の肉、骨が楽器のように、男の泣き声に共振れをおこしていたことが、不思議だった。梢から、湿気が水玉となって落ちていた。ぽと、ぽと、音がした。「あと、一時間もすれば、川に出ます。川沿いを歩けば、村にいきつきます」

一五「救けは受けとうない、このまま置き去りにして下され、それともいっそ殺してくれ」

「あなたは誰なのですか?」彼は訊いた。男は黙った。弱くわらう声がきこえた。

「おれが誰であろうかよ。この山に這いまわる乞食、かったいの仲間よ」男は言った。「名前などない」

「あなたを救けたい」

一六「馬鹿げたことを言って」男は、言った。声が闇の中で、響いた。日はすっかり落ちてしまっていた。さっきまでおぼろげにみえていた杉の木の形も、いまはなかった。滴がしきりに落ちていた。「それよりもいっそこのおれを殺してくれ。この先何年も何年も、こんな体で生きていくのは心苦しい。殺してくれ」男は言った。

「ほれ」と言葉をつぎ、黙った。「聞えるか、村の方から、また、おれを呼ぶ」男は言った。彼の耳にも声は、聞えた。方々から、老若男女のものらしいいくつもいくつもの声が掛る。その声の波に合わせて、山が、ざわざわと音をたてる。梢がうごき、彼の足を置いたあたりの草が、むずむずと身をもちあげる。地面がぼこぼこっと音をたてて動く。ふっと息苦しくなる。「ほれ、あの声。あの声があるために、夜は寝れない」彼は聞いた。それはまぎれもなく、母の声だった。姉たちの声だった。「里の村へおりて行って、言ってくれ。もう苦しむな、もう忘れろ、と。いまさら母が苦しんでなんになる。嫁いでいった妹たちが苦しんで、なんになる。母や妹たちを苦しめるために、くびれたんではない。母や妹たちが幸せになるように、くびれた。おれのことは忘れて、幸せに生きろ」

[一七]「その代り、あんたが、左眼を潰され、左脚を損じて苦しんでいる」

「おれのことはいい」男は黙る。「だから、おれは頼んでいる。男のお前に。殺してくれ」

[一八]　その時、声がした。それは、姉の声だった。「兄やんねえ、覚えとるかあ」と聞えた。それから母の声もした。母は、呻いていた。「おまえが、首つって、すぐ家に運び込まれ、母さんが顔みたら、赤い鼻血がたらたら出てきたねえ。かわいいもんよ。なんで若い身空で首つって死んだ？みんな、母さんが悪かった。母さんが一番悪かった」母は泣く。

[一九]「おれは、おまえを救ける」彼は言った。立ちあがった。男の腕をつかもうとした。「要らん」と男は振り払った。ざわざわと音がした。梢が鳴った。喉を圧し潰し痛みに耐えきれぬ呻きをあげた。おう、おう、とけもののように男は唸った。彼の耳のそばで誰かがむっくりと起きあがる気配がし、ひた、ひた、ひたと音をたてて、木立

の下を歩いていく。「ああ、かわいもんよ、なんで死んだ」母の声に合わせるように、男は、おう、おう、と呻く。「もう忘れてくれ。人の世に生れなんだら、よかった。忘れてくれ」彼は、痛みを耐えきれぬ男の呻き声を耳にし、その小さいものの、ひくひくとうごく赤い肉を思い出した。なにもわからず、なにひとつ知らず、生命は風にさらされ光にさらされ、うごく。あれは、兄の生れ変りか？「里の村で、母に伝えてくれ。なにひとつ苦しむな、忘れろと。病に苦しめられ、そのうえに、死んだ子の齢をかぞえて苦しんで、なんになる。母が泣く。妹の、泣く声がする。死んだ者を想うことは要らん。器量よしのその顔が、台無しになる。生きよ。身も心も魂も夫に預け、兄のことは忘れろ。生きてくれ」彼の眼に涙がたまる。凍りついた闇の中で、彼はいま、十何年前に死んだ兄と向い合って杉の根方に坐り込み、しゃべっている。あれから、死をまっとうに死ぬことも出来ず、こうやって傷つき山中にうずくまっていたのか？

二〇

法事を終え、東京にもどってきた彼は、その盲いて生れた小鳥が、雑居籠の四つほどある巣の一つに足をひっかけ、干乾べて死んでいるのをみつけたのだった。まさに、殻断ちを行ったのと一緒だった。足にまきついた糸をほどき、手のひらに乗せてみた。彼はしばらくそうやって固く干乾びたそいつをみていた。日の光が、へんに優しいのを知ったのだった。

## CORNELL EAST ASIA SERIES

4 Fredrick Teiwes, *Provincial Leadership in China: The Cultural Revolution and Its Aftermath*
8 Cornelius C. Kubler, *Vocabulary and Notes to Ba Jin's Jia: An Aid for Reading the Novel*
16 Monica Bethe & Karen Brazell, *Nō as Performance: An Analysis of the Kuse Scene of Yamamba*
17 Royall Tyler, tr., *Pining Wind: A Cycle of Nō Plays*
18 Royall Tyler, tr., *Granny Mountains: A Second Cycle of Nō Plays*
23 Knight Biggerstaff, *Nanking Letters, 1949*
28 Diane E. Perushek, ed., *The Griffis Collection of Japanese Books: An Annotated Bibliography*
37 J. Victor Koschmann, Ōiwa Keibō & Yamashita Shinji, eds., *International Perspectives on Yanagita Kunio and Japanese Folklore Studies*
38 James O'Brien, tr., *Murō Saisei: Three Works*
40 Kubo Sakae, *Land of Volcanic Ash: A Play in Two Parts,* revised edition, tr. David G. Goodman
44 Susan Orpett Long, *Family Change and the Life Course in Japan*
48 Helen Craig McCullough, *Bungo Manual: Selected Reference Materials for Students of Classical Japanese*
49 Susan Blakeley Klein, *Ankoku Butō: The Premodern and Postmodern Influences on the Dance of Utter Darkness*
50 Karen Brazell, ed., *Twelve Plays of the Noh and Kyōgen Theaters*
51 David G. Goodman, ed., *Five Plays by Kishida Kunio*
52 Shirō Hara, *Ode to Stone,* tr. James Morita
53 Peter J. Katzenstein & Yutaka Tsujinaka, *Defending the Japanese State: Structures, Norms and the Political Responses to Terrorism and Violent Social Protest in the 1970s and 1980s*
54 Su Xiaokang & Wang Luxiang, *Deathsong of the River: A Reader's Guide to the Chinese TV Series* Heshang, trs. Richard Bodman & Pin P. Wan
55 Jingyuan Zhang, *Psychoanalysis in China: Literary Transformations, 1919-1949*
56 Jane Kate Leonard & John R. Watt, eds., *To Achieve Security and Wealth: The Qing Imperial State and the Economy, 1644-1911*
57 Andrew F. Jones, *Like a Knife: Ideology and Genre in Contemporary Chinese Popular Music*
58 Peter J. Katzenstein & Nobuo Okawara, *Japan's National Security: Structures, Norms and Policy Responses in a Changing World*
59 Carsten Holz, *The Role of Central Banking in China's Economic Reforms*
60 Chifumi Shimazaki, *Warrior Ghost Plays from the Japanese Noh Theater: Parallel Translations with Running Commentary*
61 Emily Groszos Ooms, *Women and Millenarian Protest in Meiji Japan: Deguchi Nao and Ōmotokyō*

62 Carolyn Anne Morley, *Transformation, Miracles, and Mischief: The Mountain Priest Plays of Kōygen*
63 David R. McCann & Hyunjae Yee Sallee, tr., *Selected Poems of Kim Namjo,* afterword by Kim Yunsik
64 Hua Qingzhao, *From Yalta to Panmunjom: Truman's Diplomacy and the Four Powers, 1945-1953*
65 Margaret Benton Fukasawa, *Kitahara Hakushū: His Life and Poetry*
66 Kam Louie, ed., *Strange Tales from Strange Lands: Stories by Zheng Wanlong,* with introduction
67 Wang Wen-hsing, *Backed Against the Sea,* tr. Edward Gunn
69 Brian Myers, *Han Sŏrya and North Korean Literature: The Failure of Socialist Realism in the DPRK*
70 Thomas P. Lyons & Victor Nee, eds., *The Economic Transformation of South China: Reform and Development in the Post-Mao Era*
71 David G. Goodman, tr., *After Apocalypse: Four Japanese Plays of Hiroshima and Nagasaki, with introduction*
72 Thomas Lyons, *Poverty and Growth in a South China County: Anxi, Fujian, 1949-1992*
74 Martyn Atkins, *Informal Empire in Crisis: British Diplomacy and the Chinese Customs Succession, 1927-1929*
76 Chifumi Shimazaki, *Restless Spirits from Japanese Noh Plays of the Fourth Group: Parallel Translations with Running Commentary*
77 Brother Anthony of Taizé & Young-Moo Kim, trs., *Back to Heaven: Selected Poems of Ch'ŏn Sang Pyŏng*
78 Kevin O'Rourke, tr., *Singing Like a Cricket, Hooting Like an Owl: Selected Poems by Yi Kyu-bo*
79 Irit Averbuch, *The Gods Come Dancing: A Study of the Japanese Ritual Dance of Yamabushi Kagura*
80 Mark Peterson, *Korean Adoption and Inheritance: Case Studies in the Creation of a Classic Confucian Society*
81 Yenna Wu, tr., *The Lioness Roars: Shrew Stories from Late Imperial China*
82 Thomas Lyons, *The Economic Geography of Fujian: A Sourcebook,* Vol. 1
83 Pak Wan-so, *The Naked Tree,* tr. Yu Young-nan
84 C.T. Hsia, *The Classic Chinese Novel: A Critical Introduction*
85 Cho Chong-Rae, *Playing With Fire,* tr. Chun Kyung-Ja
86 Hayashi Fumiko, *I Saw a Pale Horse and Selections from Diary of a Vagabond,* tr. Janice Brown
87 Motoori Norinaga, *Kojiki-den, Book 1,* tr. Ann Wehmeyer
88 Chang Soo Ko, tr., *Sending the Ship Out to the Stars: Poems of Park Je-chun*
89 Thomas Lyons, *The Economic Geography of Fujian: A Sourcebook,* Vol. 2
90 Brother Anthony of Taizé, tr., Midang: *Early Lyrics of So Chong-Ju*
92 Janice Matsumura, *More Than a Momentary Nightmare: The Yokohama Incident and Wartime Japan*
93 Kim Jong-Gil tr., *The Snow Falling on Chagall's Village: Selected Poems of Kim Ch'un-Su*

94 Wolhee Choe & Peter Fusco, trs., *Day-Shine: Poetry by Hyon-jong Chong*
95 Chifumi Shimazaki, *Troubled Souls from Japanese Noh Plays of the Fourth Group*
96 Hagiwara Sakutarō, *Principles of Poetry (Shi no Genri),* tr. Chester Wang
97 Mae J. Smethurst, *Dramatic Representations of Filial Piety: Five Noh in Translation*
98 Ross King, ed., *Description and Explanation in Korean Linguistics*
99 William Wilson, *Hōgen Monogatari: Tale of the Disorder in Hōgen*
100 Yasushi Yamanouchi, J. Victor Koschmann and Ryūichi Narita, eds., *Total War and 'Modernization'*
101 Yi Ch'ŏng-jun, *The Prophet and Other Stories,* tr. Julie Pickering
102 S.A. Thornton, *Charisma and Community Formation in Medieval Japan: The Case of the Yugyō-ha (1300-1700)*
103 Sherman Cochran, ed., *Inventing Nanjing Road: Commercial Culture in Shanghai, 1900-1945*
104 Harold M. Tanner, *Strike Hard! Anti-Crime Campaigns and Chinese Criminal Justice, 1979-1985*
105 Brother Anthony of Taizé & Young-Moo Kim, trs., *Farmers' Dance: Poems by Shin Kyŏng-nim*
106 Susan Orpett Long, ed., *Lives in Motion: Composing Circles of Self and Community in Japan*
107 Peter J. Katzenstein, Natasha Hamilton-Hart, Kozo Kato, & Ming Yue, *Asian Regionalism*
108 Kenneth Alan Grossberg, *Japan's Renaissance: The Politics of the Muromachi Bakufu*
109 John W. Hall & Toyoda Takeshi, eds., *Japan in the Muromachi Age*
110 Kim Su-Young, Shin Kyong-Nim, Lee Si-Young; *Variations: Three Korean Poets;* trs. Brother Anthony of Taizé & Young-Moo Kim
111 Samuel Leiter, *Frozen Moments: Writings on* Kabuki, *1966-2001*
112 Pilwun Shih Wang & Sarah Wang, *Early One Spring: A Learning Guide to Accompany the Film Video* February
113 Thomas Conlan, *In Little Need of Divine Intervention: Scrolls of the Mongol Invasions of Japan*
114 Jane Kate Leonard & Robert Antony, eds., *Dragons, Tigers, and Dogs: Qing Crisis Management and the Boundaries of State Power in Late Imperial China*
115 Shu-ning Sciban & Fred Edwards, eds., *Dragonflies: Fiction by Chinese Women in the Twentieth Century*
116 David G. Goodman, ed., *The Return of the Gods: Japanese Drama and Culture in the 1960s*
117 Yang Hi Choe-Wall, *Vision of a Phoenix: The Poems of Hŏ Nansŏrhŏn*
118 Mae J. Smethurst and Christina Laffin, eds., *The Noh* Ominameshi*: A Flower Viewed from Many Directions*
119 Joseph A. Murphy, *Metaphorical Circuit: Negotiations Between Literature and Science in Twentieth-Century Japan*

120 Richard F. Calichman, *Takeuchi Yoshimi: Displacing the West*

121 *Visions for the Masses: Chinese Shadow Plays from Shaanxi and Shanxi,* by Fan Pen Li Chen

122 S. Yumiko Hulvey, *Sacred Rites in Moonlight: Ben no Naishi Nikki*

123 Tetsuo Najita and J. Victor Koschmann, *Conflict in Modern Japanese History: The Neglected Tradition*

124 Naoki Sakai, Brett de Bary, & Iyotani Toshio, eds., *Deconstructing Nationality*

125 Judith N. Rabinovitch and Timothy R. Bradstock, *Dance of the Butterflies: Chinese Poetry from the Japanese Court Tradition*

126 Yang Gui-ja, *Contradictions,* trs. Stephen Epstein and Kim Mi-Young

127 Ann Sung-hi Lee, *Yi Kwang-su and Modern Korean Literature:* Mujŏng

128 Pang Kie-chung & Michael D. Shin, eds., *Landlords, Peasants, & Intellectuals in Modern Korea*

129 Joan R. Piggott, ed., *Capital and Countryside in Japan, 300-1180: Japanese Historians Interpreted in English*

130 Kyoko Selden and Jolisa Gracewood, eds., *Annotated Japanese Literary Gems: Stories by Tawada Yōko, Nakagami Kenji, and Hayashi Kyōko* (Vol. 1)

131 Michael G. Murdock, *Disarming the Allies of Imperialism: The State, Agitation, and Manipulation during China's Nationalist Revolution, 1922-1929*

Order online: www.einaudi.cornell.edu/eastasia/CEASbooks, or contact Cornell East Asia Series Distribution Center, 95 Brown Road, Box 1004, Ithaca, NY 14850, USA; toll-free: 1-877-865-2432, fax 607-255-7534, ceas@cornell.edu

*This book is printed Japanese-style, with pages ordered from right to left. This is the end of the book.*

IBT/6-06/0.5M pb/.2M hc